TRA
OUTER SPACE TO
MYSTERIOUS PLUTO...

Come to this tiny planet, our most distant neighbor, and meet the three sexes—Male, Female, and…Neuter. Love was nearly a crime on this strange planet.   A maiden's most cherished desire was to become a Neuter. Marriage—to a Plutonian maiden—was a disaster, and "love" a catastrophe to be avoided at all costs…

Packed to the hilt with outer space and inner space adventure, Stanton A. Coblentz's INTO PLUTONIAN DEPTHS is a science-fiction classic that will keep you amazed from the first to the last page, as you read of the topsy-turvy world two billion miles away where love is a lost chord in their unearthly symphony of life.

CAST OF CHARACTERS

DAN
He traveled to faraway Pluto, where he found himself a prisoner in an underground world, ruled by a fantastic alien race.

ZANDAYE
This beautiful Plutonian girl was the essence of female charm, but she thought the goal of womanhood was to join the third sex.

ANDREW STARK
He was a courageous inventor and explorer from Earth—and he dared to challenge the mixed-up morality of a distant planet.

THE HEAD SURGEON
Two Earthlings on Pluto were the cause of endless problems, but this esteemed surgeon had a solution—cut out half their brains!

THE PLUTONIAN STATESMAN
It was his job to interview two visiting Earthlings—and he was quick to point out that their home planet couldn't possibly exist.

THE HEAD NEUTER
Ruler of the bizarre inner world of Pluto. His decision was to severely punish Zandaye—by forcing her to remain a woman!

THE LAMP-HEADS
The strange race of people who inhabited the inside world of Pluto, who had light bulbs growing in their skulls, and who thought that any race without three sexes must be abnormal.

INTO PLUTONIAN DEPTHS

By STANTON A. COBLENTZ

ARMCHAIR FICTION
PO Box 4369, Medford, Oregon 97504

*For more information about Armchair Books and products, visit our
website at…*

www.armchairfiction.com

Or email us at…

armchairfiction@yahoo.com

PART ONE

CHAPTER ONE
The Great Discovery

ANDREW LYMAN STARK and I stood staring at one another across the brilliant metallic glitter of the laboratory. If appearances had not deceived, we had made one of the great discoveries of all time.

However, let me go back and tell how it all came about. If we had achieved a revolutionary find, at least it had come to us by no accident, and was no more than we had been struggling to accomplish as far back as I can remember.

Yes, as far back as I can remember the problem had been in my mind. I shall never forget how, as a small boy, I was fascinated by the stars, and the thought that they were far-off worlds; and how, with a small boy's sense of the adventurous, I began to wonder how it would feel to go sailing across the skies and set foot on some other universe. Of course, I was encouraged at first by the tales of Jules Verne, H. G. Wells and other romancers; but, subsequently, prolonged and serious scientific study convinced me that interplanetary travel was possible. After my graduation from college, when I obtained a position as Instructor in Astronomy, I took advantage of the well-equipped library and observatory of Clayton University to further my plans and investigations.

From the beginning, however, I was aided and encouraged in everything by my boon companion and fellow worker, Andy Stark, without whom neither the conception nor execution of my grandiose scheme would have been possible. From childhood he had been my friend; we had grown up together in the same little country town; he had shared my boyhood enthusiasms and delights; my dreams had been his dreams, and his dreams mine; and I can well remember how, at the ripe age of twelve, the two of us would sit together of a summer's evening on some broken fence beside a cornfield and gravely plan the heroic deeds to be performed after a flight to some neighboring world.

His picture as he was on that day when we exulted together at our first triumph, frames itself vividly in my imagination: his round, sun-tanned face, dominated by blue eyes that seemed to bubble from inexhaustible springs of laughter; his broad forehead surmounted by a crop of wavy light hair that never was and never could be in order; his thin lips which habitually took a humorous or satiric slant and yet did not belie the serious expression that dominated the face; his carelessly adjusted garments, always overlarge, always flung about the tall frame as loosely as old sacks.

Even after our college days, it was as if we had a twin destiny, for no sooner did I become Instructor in Astronomy than Stark received an appointment as Instructor in Physics in the same University. And so once more we took rooms together, and were collaborators in our plans and experiments.

Several years now went by without bearing visible fruit: other than in the depression and discouragement that preceded the eventual discovery. By the time of our graduation, Stark and I had agreed that the possibility of leaving the Earth and traveling to another planet depended upon one factor and one alone—the force of gravity. Gravity at the earth's surface, you will recall, is so powerful that a projectile, unless propelled by some vast source of energy, would have to attain a speed of almost seven miles a second in order to be released into outer space. There was, however, one conceivable alternative: that we should rise in defiance of gravity. And it was in this direction that all our hopes lay.

I must here give Stark credit for a brilliant theory, although one in which he was not alone, for something like it was announced a little later by no less an authority than Einstein.

"I don't look upon gravitation as an isolated force," I remember my friend remarking one evening, as he lounged across from me among the pillows of a disordered divan. "Rather, I believe it will be found some day to be linked to magnetism and electricity. Gravitation, magnetism, and electricity—think carefully about those three, Dan, for—who knows—they may hold the secret of the universe. Personally, I've a notion that gravity is not an absolute and unalterable force, which operates in all circumstances, and always in the same manner, according to the laws of Newton. No other such force is known in nature; heat, light, electricity, kinetic energy, are all subject to change and regulation according to the principles which we create for them; even radioactivity is to be found only under rare and restricted circumstances; while magnetism is limited to particular metals. Why, therefore, should gravity alone not be susceptible of control? Why shouldn't there be substances over which it has little or no influence? True, no such substances have ever been discovered; but that thought shouldn't deter us in our search for a gravity insulator."

"Gravity insulator?" I repeated, sitting up in my armchair with excited interest. "Gravity insulator, did you say?"

"Yes, gravity insulator. After all, is there anything really surprising in the idea? You're pretty well acquainted with electric insulators, aren't you? Doesn't it ever strike you as odd that a lineman, equipped with rubber gloves, may safely handle a wire charged with current enough to electrocute him? We can only theorize why it is that electricity will dart through one solid substance practically without resistance, while another substance, no more solid to our eyes, will oppose it like a wall of adamant. However, we do know that such things happen and we continually take advantage of the fact. And so why not take advantage of similar facts with regard to gravity? If gravity is related to electricity in essence, we should be able to build an insulator against both alike."

A moment later, seated side by side on the couch, while his great eyes sparkled with a contagious joy, we plunged into an eager discussion of ways and means of finding the gravity annihilator.

Now that I look back upon our years of blundering experimentation, it seems extraordinary that we should ever have found a gravity insulator. Even though theoretically we were on the right track, in practice our difficulty was a little like that of retrieving a lost pearl from a wilderness of brambles. Somewhere in the universe, we were convinced, there existed a substance—possibly many substances—through which gravity could not operate; yet neither Stark nor I had more than the vaguest idea where to find that substance. Our only clue in the beginning was to follow the analogy of electricity: if gravity and electricity were related, then possibly some material that was an exceedingly poor conductor of the one would prove also immune to the other. And so, for more than two years, we experimented, testing every substance of high electrical resistance, and even originating numbers of new chemical compounds; but we might as well have sat twiddling our fingers.

We would have been less than human had we not been discouraged. Yet in us both there was some dogged quality that did not permit us to give up easily; and so, even when hope had all but left us, we persisted, and performed new computations, and stained our hands with new chemicals, and formulated new plans of attack. But doubtless we would ultimately have surrendered—had not the goddess of chance, or what we like to call chance, smiled upon us unexpectedly...

I remember that one morning Stark was experimenting with a new asbestos compound, and had expressed his intention of subjecting it to the X-ray in the hope of getting a "degravitating effect." Why he hoped to get such an effect; or why he used the X-ray at all, or used it upon this particular substance, I have never learned; while his only explanation is that he was struck by a "happy intuition." In any case, I do know that, when he announced his plans, I merely shrugged, convinced that he was following one more blind alley. So I was really surprised when, two or three hours later, I peeped in at the door of our little laboratory, and found Stark bent over a table and a pair of scales with trance-like absorption. It was some time before he became aware of my presence; and as I stood silently at the door, and observed how intently his eyes were concentrated upon the objects of his experiment, and how his fingers trembled and his whole frame quivered, I too began to grow excited.

"Andy!" I murmured, no longer able to endure the suspense.

He started toward me like a man who has been struck. "Dan! Why, I—I didn't know you were here," he muttered, apologetically. "You—you gave me such a shock!"

Then, after a moment of silence, his eyes were animated by an eloquent light; his whole face was swept by a wave of exultant joy. "You're just in time, Dan," he exclaimed, seizing my hand and almost dragging me into the laboratory. "Come—see!"

He reached toward the table, and thrust into my hand an iron bar weighing three or four pounds. "Just feel this," he ordered.

I did as commanded, and remarked that the iron bar seemed an ordinary one.

"Now lift the rod over here…" he directed, pointing to the table, on which lay a grayish-green sheet of the asbestos compound.

Wonderingly, I obeyed directions. But what magic was this? What an eerie sensation overcame me. I shuddered, and trembled in every limb; a chill crept down my spine; I had the feeling of one who has seen a ghost. All at once, it was as if half the iron rod had been drawn from my hands; I was conscious of only half its former weight!

"You see!" cried Stark, pacing rapidly back and forth, while fairly boiling over with delight. "It works! It *works!* The gravity insulator!"

I shall not attempt a detailed account of the experiments of the next two or three months. That chance discovery of Stark's—that the action of the X-ray would partly degravitize the asbestos compound—provided a working basis that made our final success only a matter of weeks. It seemed highly unlikely that Stark, at that first lucky stroke, had hit upon the ideal degravitizing compound; and further experiments showed us, indeed, that by varying the proportions, introducing new ingredients, and prolonging the action of the X-ray, it was possible to increase the resistance to gravity and to make any substance lose not merely one half, but two thirds, three quarters, or even nine tenths of its original weight! This, of course, was encouraging, but not sufficient; for so long as gravity acted at all, it would be difficult to surmount it. However, we already had the key; it was now only a question of refining our gravity insulator, of removing all impurities susceptible to the earth's attraction. And this task was one of patient plodding and testing until in the end we had an insulator that, weightless itself, would immunize any object above it to the earth's attraction.

And so at last there came a day when, placing our hands above the screen of contragrav—as we had termed our invention—we could detect no weight whatever. It was as if our flesh and blood did not exist; we could hold our hands in air as easily as we could rest them on the table; while any small object—whether a feather or a piece of lead—might remain uncannily floating above the contragrav, as though in defiance of Newton.

"It's done! At last—at last we can fly to the stars." Stark bubbled over and, with my hands clasped in his, he began to do. A wild dance about the room, scarcely noticing how many books or scientific implements he upset...

It was sheer exhaustion that bade him finally halt, and, panting and happy, fling himself into a chair across from me. How flushed his face was. How disheveled his long, wild hair. How brilliant the light in his scintillate blue eyes!

"There's no reason for delay now," he rattled forth, when he had recovered his breath. "We'll complete our plans at once. We'll make our computations—build a car of contragrav! Within six months, Dan, if all goes well—within six months, we'll set sail for some other planet."

"Within six months!" I echoed enthusiastically.

Why was it that, despite my exultation, a momentary shudder came across me? Why was it that I trembled, and felt vaguely uneasy? Why was it that, a term of six months having been definitely set, I experienced a sudden revulsion, an unreasoning repugnance, almost a flash of terror?

CHAPTER TWO
The Wanderer of the Skies

WHEN STARK predicted that our great adventure would have begun within six months, he was letting his enthusiasm run away with his sense of scientific possibility. Not six months but a year was the minimum time that we found necessary; in fact, considerably over a year was required, while our days were passed in nervous expectation, delirious planning, and slow plodding labor.

Taking advantage of a considerable fortune that I had recently inherited, we contracted with a leading iron works to construct a spherical car of reinforced and tempered steel—a car about seventy feet in diameter and fitted out according to curious specifications. The metallic envelope was to be encased in a thick layer of contragrav; and this substance was to be provided in one hundred closely fitting although separable segments, all of which were to be under control by means of springs and wires, so that the occupant of the car could cause any of them to fold out of place or return to place merely by pulling the proper switch. This, as will presently be seen, was of high importance, for our chief motive power was to be the gravitational pull of the planets and the sun, which could be regulated by exposing any particular part of the car to the attraction of any desired heavenly body.

Next in importance I rank two powerful gasoline engines (likewise enclosed in contragrav,) which were to send us skyward at an initial velocity of several hundred miles an hour. Beyond the limits of the earth's atmosphere, they would of course be useless until we struck the atmosphere of some other planet; while the huge propeller blades would have offered a serious obstacle in outer space had Stark not invented a little device compelling them to withdraw automatically behind layers of contragrav as soon as we reached the upper atmosphere.

I shall not list all of the provisions and scientific instruments which we held necessary for our flight: the case upon case of concentrated food, the barrels of distilled water, the oxygen generators, the navigational apparatus, the thermometers, barometers, telescopes, and other paraphernalia; the medical apparatus and surgical implements, the storage batteries for producing light and heat, the radio apparatus to signal the earth, the gas-masks to provide us temporarily with oxygen in case that essential gas was lacking at our destination, the library of pocket-sized books for filling the many, many idle hours en route… Let me pass over all this, to turn to the thing upon which all this largely depended.

Before we could determine the details of our outfit, we had to decide upon our goal. And this, for a long time, provided a bone of contention. My original suggestion was that we make a modest beginning, and travel to the moon. Being less than a quarter of a million miles away, our satellite would provide the most convenient destination; a few days, and we would be there! And the prospects of returning would be far better than if we had sought the wilds of the outer universe. However, Stark would have nothing of this idea. "What? Only go to the moon?" he cried, his big eyes darting indignation. "Why, that would be only like a trip to the suburbs. Once we've set out, we might as well make a real voyage. Sirius…Arcturus…the nebula in Andromeda!"

"Come, come, Andy, you know you're raving." I said firmly; and, indeed, a faint mischievous twinkle in his eyes showed that he was not wholly in earnest. "You realize as well as I do that the nearest fixed star is more than three light years away. Even traveling at one hundred and eighty-six thousand miles a second—which, you will admit, is fast enough—it would take us over three years!"

Stark gave a dry chuckle, and mopped his long hair thoughtfully.

"Well, I suppose I would get a little impatient, waiting that long," he muttered. "Guess, after all, we'd better try Venus, Mercury, or Mars."

"All right, then, let's decide upon Mars."

Stark grunted, and Mars would undoubtedly have been our destination—had it not been for the caprices of my incalculable comrade. It happened at about this time that he read an article on the trans-Neptunian planet Pluto. And the effect of the article upon Stark was overwhelming. Something in the very name of Pluto, something in the thought of this forlorn ninth member of the Solar System, took an irresistible hold upon his imagination, and for days he seemed able to talk about little else.

"Think of this strange, strange world!" he would exclaim, while he would pace up and down the room and stroke his chin as though weighing some momentous problem. "Think of it a billion miles or so beyond Neptune, perhaps no larger than the earth, lost in the blackness of the outer void, its years longer than our centuries, its seasons longer than our lives! What stories it would be able to tell! Are there any living creatures there? Were living beings ever able to endure the terror of its sunless plains. Would we find the imprint of lost races upon its shores? Races that flourished while the planet was heated from within? Just consider, Dan—consider the scientific value of exploring such a world. May its geological strata not hold the secret of evolution? Yes, the secret of the evolution of the universe?"

It seemed to me that Stark, in bursting into such

rhapsodies, was guilty of the wildest, most irrational extravagance. None the less, how could I listen and remain unaffected? Gradually, in spite of myself—in spite of the protests of my own reason—I was coming to hear him with a gathering interest, a heightened pleasure; gradually I too began to draw pictures of the joy of descending upon that remote sun-forsaken world. And by degrees, without exactly realizing it myself, I was capitulating, capitulating before Stark's emotional fervor…

Nevertheless, the final concession was not made until after long debate. Stemming the tides of our enthusiasm, I had performed some sober calculations; and the results were not of a nature to make me shout with joy. On the basis of the computed distance of Pluto, it would take us nearly a year to arrive even if we were to travel at an average speed of one hundred and fifty miles a second. One hundred and fifty miles a second! Few of the heavenly bodies were known to attain such velocity. And one year of travel—one year locked in a tiny flying cage. Even my lifelong longing for interplanetary travel wavered before such a prospect.

And yet my intended fellow voyager, when I put the problem before him, seemed not at all disturbed.

"Yes, I've considered all that," he declared. "Have you made any precise computations of the possibilities of our contragrav car? Well, I have. You've seen speeds of three hundred miles a second or over attributed to certain of the stars and nebulae; but the reason that twenty or thirty miles is seldom exceeded in the Solar System is that gravity acts by checks and balances; the pull of one planet counteracts that of another. Now, in our contragrav car, all that will be changed. We'll be subject to gravity in the direction we choose, and in that direction only; there will be no checks and balances. If we're subjected to the pull of Pluto, for example, not only Pluto, but all the myriads of stars far, far in the background will draw us on. On the other hand, the stars to our rear will be as if they didn't exist. And thus, Dan, we may travel three hundred miles a second, and reach Pluto in a little more than seven months. It will be possible, as you know, to exist that long in our car."

"Even so," I objected, "I can't see how that solves the problem. Traveling at three hundred miles a second, how can we halt our flight?"

Stark stared at me as if wondering whether I could be serious.

"Have you forgotten," he demanded, "our arrangements for the use of contragrav? Suppose, we're within thirty or forty million miles of Pluto, which we're approaching at several hundred miles a second? All we'll have to do will be to close the contragrav windows on the side of Pluto, which will cut off the attraction of that planet; and open the contragrav windows on the side of the sun, which will let in the sun's attraction and gradually slow us down to any speed we desire."

"Hope it'll be as easy as it sounds," I grunted; and the debate came to a close. However, we both knew he had triumphed.

* * *

As the time of our flight approached, we were conscious of a growing uneasiness. Even though we tried our best to shut out dreary reflections, both Stark and I acted like men under sentence of death. We made our wills; we put our affairs in order; we secured indefinite leaves of absence from the University; we left instructions that if, five years from the date of our departure, we had not been seen or heard of, our property was to be devoted to certain institutions for the advancement of science. Luckily, neither of us had any dependents; we were both unmarried, our parents were dead, our brothers and sisters well able to fend for themselves—therefore our lives seemed our own to risk. True, at times I noticed a dimming of Stark's eyes as I mentioned a certain lively, black-haired girl; but, if he was unable to keep a pained expression from his face, he would at least grit his teeth with grim-featured resolution.

Months in advance, our date of departure had been set for the first of May; while the place of departure was to be a little field about five miles from the iron works—a field to which our car, despite its size, could easily be removed because of its weightless condition. As for the date, it had been chosen after careful computations; on the first of May the position of the heavenly bodies would be such as to permit us to set out with a minimum of difficulty. Our particular point of departure, of course, was a matter of little consequence; but the chosen field had the advantage of being several miles from town, and hence unlikely to attract a crowd.

When at length the day arrived, Stark and I arose early after an almost sleepless night. We bathed and dressed in silence; we tossed down a cup or two of coffee that seemed strangely tasteless to our lips; then, leaving our toast and eggs untouched, we stepped into the waiting automobile. As we sped across the fresh green fields and around the bends of blossoming hills, we thought how soon we were to make a vastly swifter flight through regions vastly stranger; and, at that reflection, a great sadness overcame us. Still cursed by this emotion, I caught my first glimpse of a spherical grayish green projection far in the distance—the contragrav car! As we drew near, I saw that an enormous crowd had gathered, motor cars were parked for half a mile on both sides of the road, making it difficult for us to approach. When the, throng became aware of our presence, however, tumultuous cheers burst forth; we were surrounded enthusiastically, lifted bodily from our seats, and borne on the shoulders of the crowd toward the interplanetary vehicle. We could see its gigantic frame swaying in the breeze, tied by ropes like a balloon; we could see its name, the *Wanderer of the Skies,* streaming from a pennant; we could see the small windows, looking little larger than human eyes, which here and there served as spy-holes in the otherwise unbroken contragrav envelope; we could see the two huge gasoline engines which lay at the base of the sphere to supply the initial motive power. However, this was all that we could see; the mob was so demonstrative that we could do little more than return their greetings and creep as speedily as possible through the little door at the base of the *Wanderer of the Skies.*

The time of departure had been set for three in the afternoon, but meanwhile there was much to be done: we had to make our final tests, to determine that the air-tight compartments were all securely closed, to examine the oxygen tubes and water tanks, and to ascertain that the straps lashing each cask and article of furniture to the floor were all properly in place. It was with a dizzy sensation, a feeling of being but half present, that I went through all these tasks; but finally they were all completed.

Watch in hand, Stark stood before me, pale but composed. "Time..." I heard him mutter.

Instantly the whirring and thudding of motors came to our ears, and the car began to quiver and vibrate like a living thing. And slowly, gradually, and so easily that at first I did not realize that we were in motion, we began to rise.

For a moment we opened one of the contragrav windows to its full width of six inches, letting in a view of the throng below. The spectators were writhing, and stamping about tumultuously, waving their arms and pointing to us wide-mouthed. However, their clamoring no longer came to our ears, and after a minute they began to grow faraway, strange, like pygmy creatures. Then, unable to endure the sight of their rapid dwindling, we slammed the window and went about the business of celestial navigation.

CHAPTER THREE
En Route

HAD ANY OF OUR friends been able to peer through the walls of our car some time later, they would have gasped in astonishment. They would have seen men who seemed equipped with occult or magical powers, men able to walk in air, men who glided from end to end of a long compartment without touching the floor! They would have gazed at human beings with bodies of a feathery lightness! No, more than of a feathery lightness! Of the impalpable fineness of disembodied spirits! No sensation could be eerier or more frightening; it was as if my physical bulk had ceased to be. Not for hours could I overcome the sense of having been "emptied out," of being only half present, or less than half present; yet when gradually I began to accustom myself to my new environment, I felt an unimaginable freedom, a delicious buoyancy and effortless ease of movement, so that I began to wonder how other men were able to endure their slow and plodding frames.

It was not, of course, that we were entirely free from gravity. The attraction of the earth had indeed been cut off by the contragrav; but we relied upon other gravitational forces. The time of departure had been nicely calculated so that the moon would be almost directly overhead; and it was the lunar power that accelerated our speed during the first hours of the flight. Then, when we were as near our satellite as safety permitted, we closed the windows looking out upon the moon, and opened the windows in the direction of Mars, by whose attraction we were to be ruled for many days. The whole process involved computations that had engaged Stark and myself for weeks; but those computations had told us to the fraction of a second how much margin we had, and how long to continue in each direction.

Inside the *Wanderer of the Skies,* every cubic inch had been utilized. There was, first of all, the main living compartment, which ran from end to end of the car in its central zone, and which, with its ten-foot ceiling, its couches, its dining table, its case of books, its scientific implements, its gymnastic appliances, was as varied in content as a museum. Beneath this room, and above it—"beneath" and "above," of course, were now only relative terms—were the storage rooms and the "oxygen laboratory"; the first laden with casks of water and case upon case of provisions, the second filled with appliances for maintaining the oxygen supply. In addition, there were enormous airtight containers for waste products; cylinders of gasoline for driving our motors in the atmosphere of Pluto; scores upon scores of electric storage batteries, charts and maps of the heavens, notebooks, electric stoves, fur coats and other Arctic apparel...

Propelled by the gasoline motors to the upper levels of the atmosphere, we were only a few minutes in attaining a velocity of three hundred and eighty miles an hour. From time to time, glancing through one of the tiny slits or windows which we drew open by the pressure of a little lever, we could see the earth out-flung far beneath us, its hills and fields gleaming in green and blue and brown, its lakes and oceans shining in silvery, burnished sheets, its eastern expanses featureless and black. It was only an hour or two before the whole globe stood revealed, a huge mass rolling amid the blaze of sunlight, with polar caps frosty and magnificent, with seas and continents streaked and banded with snowy clouds.

Swifter and swifter we soared; four hundred, five hundred, six hundred, seven hundred miles an hour was registered by the speed gauge; yet, once we had surmounted the atmosphere, shut off the gasoline engines and folded the propeller blades behind contragrav screens, our car showed no more vibration than if chained to the everlasting rock.

For hours it was as if we were falling directly down upon the moon; so that in time it became a little frightening to see its huge grim craters drawing near as if to consume us. While I had all confidence in our computations, I really was a little relieved when the moment came for changing our course. What if, for some unforeseen reason, our contragrav screens had failed at a crucial time?

But on and on we glided during the days that followed; on and on through the silence and emptiness, the earth now a dot behind us, the ruddy orb of Mars looming ahead, while the sun's disk was narrowing and its light and heat were growing visibly less. Then, when we were within a few million miles of our neighbor world, we rearranged the openings in the contragrav and adjusted ourselves to the attraction of Saturn (Jupiter was now on the opposite side of the sun). Our speed by this time was tremendous—well over a hundred miles a second, and constantly being accelerated.

Yet more than six weeks were to pass before the ringed planet stared at us from a distance of twenty or thirty million miles and we shifted our course so as to be drawn forward by Uranus. During the interval, we had been occupied with our computations, with our scientific instruments, with telescopic observations, with our daily notes and a detailed "log" of the cruise—and with sheer ennui. However, it was the ennui, I believe, that came out first. There were our books, of course, but the earth life they depicted seemed so remote. Again, there were the gymnastic appliances—but our exercises were weird and fantastic affairs now that we were almost weightless. Then there were our attempts to signal the Earth by radio, though we had no receiver of sufficient power and could not know whether our signals were heard; and, finally, there were our long, long talks, when Stark would sit across from me, neither of us smoking, since we must conserve our oxygen, but the two of us vying in plans for accomplishment and discovery on Pluto.

Meanwhile the strain upon our nerves was harrowing. Even though our flight was progressing favorably, the long, monotonous pilgrimage might have proved fatal to any comradeship less strongly cemented than ours. Despite ourselves, and for no reason that we could explain, we would have fits of querulousness and irritability; we would sulk, glower, and be ready to take fire at any chance action or remark. And this was not due only to the monotony and the solitude—it sprang of something ominous and depressing in the very atmosphere about us, something inimical and deadly, as though demoniac forces brooded unseen in the sheer emptiness of our surroundings. As human beings accustomed to a warm, blazing sun, we could not easily endure the utter blackness of space; we could not reconcile ourselves to the sight of the diminishing solar orb.

However, let me pass over those months, except for the terrible culmination. Somehow—since there was no choice—Stark and I endured the ordeal; somehow we retained our sanity as we went gliding into the void beyond Uranus; then as we swept onward for many, many more weeks, beyond the orbit of Neptune; then further, further, further still, down into the terrible abyss, in a flight more dreadful than ever a Dante pictured for an imaginary Inferno. Far ahead, hundreds and hundreds of millions of miles in the distance, the vague form of Pluto was visible to our telescopes, though scarcely larger to the naked eye than a star of the sixth magnitude—and straight down toward this elusive goal we went rushing at a speed that would have circumnavigated the earth in little more than a minute.

By the time that we had come within close range of Pluto—which is to say, within a hundred million miles or so—our telescopes clearly showed us its disk, silvery gray and forlorn amid the star-littered blackness, I may compare its appearance to that of a second and paler moon: feebly illuminated by the far-off sunlight, it showed but indistinctly the dark markings that we took to be mountain ranges, and the lighter spaces that were perhaps frozen plains. All about us was a somberness as of late twilight; the sun, a brilliant point whole infinities behind us, seemed of less than the width of a pea; seemed little more than an exceptionally bright star shining among the myriads of stars. Had it not been for the electric lights, we would have been unable to do more than grope about the darkness even had the walls of our car been of glass.

It was when we were careering through the gloomy outer void—when we had been seven months on our way and only an eight days' flight remained to us—that an event occurred which might have precluded the writing of these memoirs.

Now that I consider all that happened, I realize that the peril was one we were constantly exposed to, one which no amount of planning would have availed against, one that might have ended our careers so swiftly that we would never have known of its existence.

One evening—or, rather, what we called "evening," for the sake of convenience—Stark and I were about to retire, when a peculiar sound, half-thudding and half hissing, attracted our attention. It was not very loud, but there was a dull, sickly quality about it that caused us to stop short in our footsteps. Strangely, it reminded me of the impact of a bullet, for it had the same startling suddenness and decisiveness.

For a moment we stood staring at one another, wondering

if the noise were to be repeated. Then, as instinctively we glanced in its apparent direction, Stark gave a low moan.

"Look! By God look, Dan!" he groaned, and darted over to where, on the opposite compartment wall, a small, crater-like bulge had appeared.

The steel about the bulge was incandescent, and our ears caught a low, sucking sound, as of air escaping.

Even in that first agitated moment, the truth was evident. We had been struck—struck at a sharp angle by a meteorite perhaps smaller than a tiny bead. But the thick steel envelope of our car had been perforated! Our precious oxygen was rushing out into vacancy!

Half an hour, an hour, two hours at most, and the greater part of our oxygen would be emptied into the hungry void, and we would gasp out our lives. So, in that first moment of horrible realization, we both imagined; and overwrought at the sight of the starlight through a small hole in the wall we found only too generous justification for terror.

Second by second the low sucking sound about the aperture became more pronounced. A faint, barely perceptible wind was blowing toward the opening, where the air, we knew, must be whirling in a miniature vortex, Stark's face had grown ghostly white.

It was Stark who broke the spell. I saw how Stark had secured the welding flame and metals—a flame which, alas! consumed still more of our oxygen. This process, too, required time—the thing we could least afford. When at last the metal was almost ready, not enough oxygen remained for good combustion. The welding flame—our chief reliance— burned feebly and low. After prolonged labors, we succeeded imperfectly in fusing a tin sheet against the metal of the wall, and so limited the escape of oxygen possibly to a small but dangerous trickle.

Now followed some of the most fear-stricken, torture-ridden hours and days of all. We were waging a life-or-death battle with suffocation, and seemed never more than a few inches in the lead. After repeated efforts, we were reconciled to the impossibility of completely sealing the cleft in the wall; and desperately we prayed that our air would hold out. Our calculations proved that we would have barely enough; if our flight should take a few hours longer than we had anticipated, we might never set foot on Pluto at all.

Thus, as the days went by, we managed barely to hold our own. Yet now we had most need of being clear-minded, for now we must make a safe landing. Guided by precious computations, we had to shut the contragrav windows on the side of Pluto at a specified hour and throw open the windows on the side of the sun, thus subjecting ourselves to a gravitational brake while still many scores of millions of miles from our destination; and we had to be sure not only that we were descending at a safe speed, but that we were gliding directly toward Pluto. Remembering the necessity of landing without waste of time, we shuddered to think how slight an error would condemn us beyond redemption.

From time to time, as Pluto came within a few millions of miles, we would draw open one of the windows for a peep at its expanding features. However, what we saw was not inviting. The broad round surface still shone with a silvery gray reflection of the sunlight, and still seemed covered with disordered, black-streaked mountain ranges and lighter-hued plains. But even with the field glasses and hand telescopes, there was no mark of life upon its monotonous, bare expanses. No cloud moved in its atmosphere; no evidence of city or forest, river or sea greeted our eager eyes; from extreme north to extreme south, the plains and mountains shone with something suspiciously white and sun reflecting.

Why, then, had we two denizens of a warmer planet come to throwaway our lives amid this frozen wilderness? Was it possible for any creature to live in that utter cold? Was there even an atmosphere capable of supporting life?

While still oppressed by such thoughts, we had to face a fresh peril. We were a little more than a day from our destination, when we noticed the oxygen gauge beginning to fall, to fall slowly and almost imperceptibly, and yet with a disquieting steadiness, I well remember with what a gray, worried face Stark set out to investigate; and how haggard was his expression when, after an hour, he hastened back to me.

"Dan! Listen…" he exclaimed, in a voice that shook though he tried to keep it composed, "the hole seems to have grown. Only a very little wider—guess from the action of the escaping air.

I stared at him. "We'll have to use the gas-masks," I exclaimed.

"Gas-masks?" echoed Stark, in tones of surprise; and immediately his face brightened with relief. "Gas-masks? Why, I hadn't thought of them! They'll help us a few hours longer."

There was no need for further speech. Both of us knew of the masks, with connecting oxygen tanks, which we had provided lest, on reaching Pluto, we should find the atmosphere unfit to breathe. We understood that those masks would enable us to live for a while in the car even should the oxygen disappear; for the gas that we generated could be emptied directly into the small storage tanks.

A few minutes later the two of us, encased in huge steel helmets and tanks, unable to eat, drink, or talk, looking ungainly as dinosaurs and feeling strange as men locked in a bottle, were able to stare about us with thankfulness and even with hope as we prepared for the crucial hours of our flight.

Those last twenty-four hours seemed as long as twenty-four days. Sleepless, hungry, unable to perform most of life's normal functions, we lived in one continuous ordeal of waiting. The steel confinement of the masks became increasingly irksome; the limited supply of oxygen made us feel like men stifling in an airtight room. All the while, we were frequently glancing at the fast-approaching Pluto, which did not rotate visibly, but seemed, like its brother Mercury, to keep one face always toward the sun. The dread of arriving too rapidly, of crashing upon its surface, was constantly with us even though we had checked each step of our mathematics repeatedly.

We had planned to come almost to a dead stop fifty or a hundred miles above the planet's surface; after which, balancing a limited amount of its gravitation against that of the sun, and aided by the gasoline engines in case there were an atmosphere, we were to descend at a leisurely rate. I rejoice to record that we actually did stop as intended although not until after encountering a resistance proving that Pluto did have an atmosphere. What type of atmosphere we could not say; yet how we longed to fling off our masks and draw a deep draught of life-giving air. However, we well knew that in these upper altitudes it would be too rarefied to breathe.

We now took but casual peeps at the approaching planet, which still showed the same wide silvery white plains as before, and the broken and enormous mountain ranges, whose snowy summits were offset by black escarpments and ravines as hideous to contemplate as the craters of the moon. As we descended, we would have been able to make out the signs of civilized life had it existed; no great city, no considerable-sized settlement could have eluded our eyes, for while the only illumination was the gray twilight shed by the sun and stars, still the frosty white nature of the surface considerably increased visibility.

Yet was it not possible that some struggling Eskimo-like

humans existed unseen amid the ice-bitten desolation?

During the last few hours of the flight, our problem was to guide ourselves to a favorable landing-place. We must descend somewhere near the Equator, where we might expect the least frigid reception; and must be careful to escape the mountains, with their terrible black gorges and crevasses. Fortunately, the plains were so wide that the second requirement was not difficult to meet; but to accomplish the first end was less easy; only by the most capable manipulation of the contragrav screens did we manage to avoid heading for the polar regions.

Yet no matter where we arrived, it would be cold enough. Hence, despite the encumbrance of the gas masks, we managed to clothe ourselves in the heavy fur coats, leggings and boots we had provided for the purpose, until we were as thoroughly muffled as any Arctic traveler. Let the temperature be fifty below, and we would be prepared.

But might the temperature not be even less than fifty below? Might it not be close to absolute zero? As I stared down at the desolate frosty expanse, I was stabbed with misgivings; at the same time, it seemed to my disordered fancy that unseen sinister forces were flitting through the gloom about us; while eerie voices, which surely were the product of delirium, cackled insanely in my ear, "Look now at dark, icy Pluto, the most forlorn planet in the universe! Look, and behold a prophecy! Read there the future of Earth! The future of *your* own Earth."

Of course, I struggled as best I could against such crazed thoughts. However, it was useless to resist. My head was in a whirl; I continued to hear voices, and to see visions; while rambling in a dream-like chaos, I gradually lost sight of the real world: of the white plains of Pluto drawing near beneath us; of the electrically lighted car, with the grotesque, mask-laden Stark laboring over the oxygen generators; of the aching pain in my breast, where the over-strained heart had been panting and laboring; of the prod of a furred boot against my leg as my companion strove time after time to rouse me back to life.

It was fortunate that Stark was able to retain some command over his dizzy brain, and to attend to the navigation in the last few miles. All at once my nerves were jarred by a terrific jolt, the walls were vibrating as from an earthquake. While I lay stunned, there came a second jolt, not quite so severe; then horrible grating and crashing sounds; and, almost at the same time, the walls quivered once more, though less convulsively; then instantly there came a third jolt...and by degrees all grew still.

Before me was a fantastic mask-bearing figure, whom I recognized only dimly. Not until he had dashed across the room, flung open the door, and disappeared in the outer void, did it come to my delirious consciousness that we had arrived!

CHAPTER FOUR
Over the Blue-White Waste

FOR A MOMENT I remained prone on the floor, struggling to recover my wits. Then, with a tremendous effort, I forced myself to my feet, and, conscious of a great weight about my shoulders and of a gravitational pull equal to that of the earth, I stumbled to the door and out to the surface of Pluto.

In that first confused glimpse, my eyes did not take in the details of the landscape. Stretching before me was a broken plain, fantastic and irregular as the floor of a glacier; huge bluish white masses, piled and tumbled together in crazy: disorder, were varied by smooth glistening flat spaces; twenty-foot mounds and hummocks stood up here and there, ands long twisted furrows or cracks spread a spidery black network across the scene; while the prevailing hue, in the wintry gray light of the far, glittering point of a sun, was that eerie, spectral mixture of blue and white, reminding me of cloud-filtered moonlight peeping down upon a lake of ice.

But all this I was to notice subsequently; in the first bewildered moment, only one thought dominated my mind: I must free myself from the gas mask, whose weight burdened my shoulders, whose confinement had nearly asphyxiated me. I must unbare my nostrils to the open winds, drink a reviving draught of actual air! True, this alien atmosphere might be poison to my lungs; true, the cold might freeze the very blood within my veins. Yet I must take the risk, I was frantic to take the risk, and clutched at the fastenings of my mask with blind desperation… Until, within a few minutes, though at first my nervous fingers would not gain any hold, I felt the burning chill of the outer air against my cheeks.

Colder than ice, the air was yet less frigid than I had expected. It did not freeze my flesh; it did not strike my lungs like poison; rather, it was the most delicious, life-giving breath I ever drew. It seemed to me that the atmosphere was lighter than on earth—light as on some high mountain peak; but it required no chemical analysis to show that it contained oxygen.

No sooner had I slipped the mask from about my shoulders and inhaled that first inexpressibly sweet breath, than I was startled to see a monstrous-looking gray form shambling from behind one of the tumbled icy projections. Certainly, my wits must still have been rambling—else I would not have jumped and let out a little half-muffled cry. In a fraction of a second I knew that this surprising shape, whom I had mistaken for some Plutonian native, was none other than Stark.

"Oh, so you're out too," he exclaimed, coming over to me in a delighted manner, while his breath congealed in ice even as he spoke, and his huge fur mittens shielded his face from the cold. "I thought I'd have trouble bringing you around."

"Oh, I'm all right," I testified, although I was shivering, and the sensation of the Arctic-type air against my ears and cheeks was beginning to be excruciating.

"Better get in here, before your face freezes," he advised, as if reading my thoughts. And he pushed me through the open doorway of the *Wanderer of the Skies,* whose electrically heated interior promised relative comfort.

"With our faces muffled in furs, we'll be able to endure the out-of-doors. Thank heaven, the temperature isn't as low as I feared," continued Stark, displaying a small thermometer. "See, only twenty-one degrees below, Fahrenheit. Why, that would be called mild and pleasant in the Antarctic."

"Why do you think it isn't lower still?" I started to ask, but checked my own words, for the answer had occurred to me. Since Pluto turned the same face always toward the sun, and since there were no clouds to interfere with the solar radiation, it enjoyed the continuous benefit of whatever sunlight was to be had at this great distance. Were similar conditions to prevail on Earth, the temperature on the lighted side would be so high that no life at all would be possible.

"Now there's just another thing," I asked. "Judging from the looks of this scenery, do you think we've come down on land? Or have we descended on a frozen sea?"

Stark twisted up his mouth into a peculiar wry grimace.

"I hope not a frozen sea—that would limit our opportunities for investigations. We'd have to go up in the *Wanderer of the Skies* again, and come down somewhere else. But let's bide our time till we find out."

I nodded; and we went about our preparations. A few minutes later, so thickly furred that only our eyes were visible amid the hairy folds of our garments, we passed out of our car, and started across the wintry plain.

Now, of all times, we should have felt elated. Yet, for some reason that I cannot explain, neither of us exulted. Stark trudged silently at my side, absorbed in his own reflections, while his breath hardened in frosty flakes upon his beard and clothes; and I, no less silent, was overcome with a violence of melancholy and nostalgia that made me bite my lips fiercely in order to keep back the tears. Perhaps it was the desolation of the scene that so affected me, the interminable, tumbled wastes with their unreal, ghostly beauty; perhaps the solitude and the silence, the knowledge that no living thing moved in the stagnant air, or crawled across the ice-sheets, or called out to mate or young. Had there been anything at all to animate the plain; had a polar bear crept out from behind some ice-block, or wolves skulked shadow-like to our rear, or some weird toothed or beaked thing scurried panic-stricken from our path, we might have shuddered, but we would have been reassured.

Glancing up at the gray, star-littered sky, with the remote gemlike sunset in one unchanging position, I asked myself what insane choice had taken us to this world of waste and silence. Should we find anything more than ice here, and further ice, with the pitiless stars gazing down upon emptiness, and the pitiless blue-white wilderness staring up at the desert sky? Now and then the swift streak of a meteor gleamed from the heavens; now and then the firmament was crossed by silken, wavering bands of light that reminded me of the aurora borealis; but except for such flashes and glimmers, it seemed to me as if this world would roll on forever without a change, without a movement, without even the sign or phantom of activity, meaning, or life.

Accordingly, it was a relief even to feel a faint pulsation in the atmosphere, to feel a weak wind arising. True, this made the cold more difficult to bear; yet we could only welcome it, even though it gradually increased in force. Nowhere, however, did the scene show any sign of a change; unending ice, varied by patches of clotted snow, made up the totality of our experience; unavailingly we looked for the footprint or relic of some living thing, the sign of some crude dwelling or hut.

Only after about an hour did we make a discovery. Suddenly we came upon a black projection with precipitous sides fifty feet high, and recognized in delight—a wall of rock!

Simultaneously we stopped short, pointing to this telltale object. "Rock!" we both exclaimed, in one breath. "We're on land!"

"On land…land…land…" I repeated, as though there

were magic in the sound. "So this isn't a frozen ocean..."

"No, though it may be only an island," exclaimed Stark. "But that isn't likely. Come, let's look more closely."

As well as we were able, we examined the cliff. Its beetling, weather-beaten sides, overhung with icicles, showed a scarred, irregular surface proving it to be some form of granite; but further features seemed to be lacking, and we were about to turn away when Stark called my attention to some peculiar markings near the base of the rock. With the aid of flashlights, we inspected them closely, much to our bewilderment—were they or were they not of natural origin? About as thick as a man's wrist, they were cut several inches into the stone in a series of jagged, perpendicular lines, giving an appearance remotely like that of hieroglyphics. Oddly enough, they had a regularity that was suggestive of human workmanship, yet were unlike any man-made markings I had ever seen.

Had they been caused merely by the scraping and tearing of the elements? Strangely, a chill, not wholly from the cold air, traveled down my spine; and my excited fancy resurrected the ghosts of the long-dead Plutonians, upon whose graves we might even now be treading.

So long did we linger examining the rock-markings that we scarcely noticed the change in the atmosphere; scarcely noticed that the breeze of a few minutes before was rising to a gale. Only when the world resounded with the intermittent screeching of a storm-wind, which howled and hooted eerily from the far-off vacancies, did we have thought of possible danger or decide to return to the *Wanderer of the Skies*.

Even so, we were not alarmed. At first Stark even found time for scientific speculations. "Come to think of it," he pointed out, as we started off together, "isn't it inevitable that Pluto should be a world of violent storms? The cold air from the unlighted side must rush with terrific power to the areas of lower pressure on the warmer side; and this must give rise to tornadoes beside which those of the earth would seem mere tempests in a teapot."

However, it was becoming painfully hard to speak and we hastened on our way without another word. Progress had suddenly grown much more difficult; the wind, sweeping about us with a surging, maniacal fury, bent our heavy, fur-laden garments as beneath an iron weight, and the numbing cold penetrated to our skins. At times, challenged by a particularly severe gust, we had to crouch behind some mound of ice, and wait for minutes before we could proceed; at other times we had to creep on hands and knees; and all the while the gale, as if possessed by some mocking demon, seemed to be growing louder, louder, fiercer, fiercer, and to beat and tear at us with shriller, more determined force. Amid the lunging fury of the elements, in which white particles of ice and snow were whirled about like sand-grains, it was difficult to find our way; indeed, we soon lost sight of our former tracks; and had it not been for the compass, which pointed toward the south, we would not have known how to retrace our course.

I cannot say whether some peculiar electrical force in the Plutonian atmosphere played havoc with the magnetic needle; or whether we had miscalculated our course, or the storm had made us lose our bearings. At all events, I know that after we had covered about a mile, we began to look expectantly for our car, but no car appeared. The very features of the landscape were unfamiliar. It seemed to us that the piles of ice were higher than before, and its surface more tumbled and irregular; that the fissures—which confronted us at frequent intervals—were wider and more dangerous, so that once or twice there was actual risk of slipping into them and being engulfed.

On and on we pushed, the storm constantly growing more

severe, our panting frames constantly nearer to exhaustion; while the cold was seeping more and more bitterly through our garments. Not yet would we admit the peril to ourselves; but we began to look still more anxiously for a certain familiar gray sphere, whose seventy-foot form, when we had last left it, had loomed conspicuously above the surrounding country.

Was it possible that the *Wanderer of the Skies* had vanished like a bubble? Was it possible that its enormous form, still more than half-covered with contragrav and hence light as a balloon, had been blown away by the storm? We did not believe so, for we had moored it with ropes. However, on the other hand we had no way of estimating the ferocity of the elements.

In any case, we caught no sight of the great machine; though after a while, with excruciating difficulty, we had advanced a distance that made it futile to continue. And so, moving ever more slowly, we began to retrace our steps, while our eyes hopelessly searched the landscape. The wind screeched and snarled more vehemently than ever, with many a gust of impish laughter; the blue-white waste spread out before us more desolate, more spectral than before, while the small flying particles beat into our eyes and impeded our progress; the dim, blinking stars and the puny, remote sun stared down at us from their same pitiless eminence; and we, crouching from time to time in some dim recess or cranny in the ice while the gale whirled and battled past, still pressed on and on, we scarcely knew whither, across the limitless, hostile solitude. Each tried as best he could to keep his feelings from the other; but with sinking hearts and scarcely audible groans, we were at last forced to admit that we were lost.

CHAPTER FIVE
In the Depths

AMID THE sweeping, whirling confusion of wind that beat down with a pummeling force, screeching more furiously and ever more furiously, progress was by yards and half yards, inches and half inches. We crawled and staggered, we slid and stumbled, we crept around exposed boulders and wormed our way on all fours through icy caves and fissures. It came to us, in a confused fashion, that perhaps our best chance would be to make ourselves a rude snow hut, in Eskimo fashion; but there was not enough free snow at hand, even if we had known how to build such a shelter; while only by keeping moving could we save ourselves from being frozen.

By this time, half blinded by the vehement gusts, we had almost given up looking for our car. Within our breasts there was such numbness and misery that we did not know or plan where we were going. Only one thing we were careful about: to keep always within sight, almost within hand's grasp of each other, for once either had lost touch with his companion, how find him again in this wailing wilderness?

Nevertheless, I was to have the shock of seeing Stark disappear. Yes, disappear literally and wholly! He had been plodding forward a yard or two ahead of me, crouching like an ape against a gale that seemed bent on blowing him away...when all at once his humped form was no longer visible. I thought that I heard a dull crash accompanied by a scream, but the pandemonium of the elements was such that

I could not be sure. All that I know is that he had slid out of sight! While stopping short and clutching my heart, I could not have been more startled had he evaporated.

Yet, almost immediately I saw that he had gone through some sort of crevasse or depression in the ice. That, however, was scarcely a consolation. What if he had plunged a thousand feet below?

It was with intense relief that, having crept forward a few paces to a large circular opening in the ice, I observed Stark in the act of picking himself up from a flat surface eight or ten feet beneath.

Evidently his fur garments had protected him from serious injury, although he was rubbing his shins in a pained manner. However, having descended, he apparently did not intend to climb out again; he motioned me to join him, and this I did after some difficulty, for even such a rude shelter would offer us relative protection.

Even to this day, I do not know what possessed Stark and me to explore that depression in the ice. About a hundred feet in diameter, with straight circular walls, its very existence was a cause for wonder; though it might have been dug by the impact of a gigantic meteorite. Why, then, did we feel an immediate, a compelling desire to study it from end to end? Shivering and miserable as we were, could we not have made ourselves temporarily secure against one of its rocky walls? But no—it was as if some guiding spirit were at hand, protecting us, leading us on, assuring us of new adventures, and providing that our voyage to Pluto should not be wholly in vain.

We had almost circumnavigated the depression, when we stopped short before a black, pit-like opening in the ice and rock. It was not more than seven feet across, and was partly blocked with an icy accumulation; but, despite this obstruction, we were immediately struck with its geometrical regularity of design. Even in the uncertain light, we could see that it formed a perfect circle, the curves much more exact than nature usually accomplishes.

Trembling at this discovery we turned our flashlights fully upon the opening. The cavity was black, black as starless space, and slanted down on an angle of forty-five degrees, but just beneath the rim, and as far down as we could see, the rock had been cut with mathematical regularity in a definite pattern! The floor was not unbroken—it reached down in a long series of steps!

Or, to be more exact, the rock had been chiseled out in blocks about a foot thick, a foot wide, and nearly three feet long; all the successive chiseling had been ordered by the same plan, with no perceptible difference in the proportions of the various steps.

For a moment, Stark and I stood stock-still and speechless. Then, of one accord, we began to examine the upper stairs in detail. They were encrusted in ice, which may have covered them for a year, a thousand years, or a thousand thousand years. Yet, from the thickness of the coating, we agreed that probably they were of ancient origin. "Maybe made by the last survivors of the Plutonians, before the cold exterminated them," suggested Stark, whose teeth chattered as he spoke. "Guess we'd better explore a bit."

I must confess that that dark, mysterious tunnel, sloping down into the bowels of the planet, did not look enticing. At the same time, our present position was little more enticing; we had found a partial shelter, but were still swept by the frigid gusts; our numbed fingers were still stiff, and the chill had not left our spines; the storm, instead of abating, was whirling above us with a howling frenzy that seemed to be on the increase, while harassing us with growing showers of small white pellets.

However, if we ventured a short distance into the tunnel,

would we not be protected? Would we not be able to pass the hours in safety until the storm subsided?

It was with this hope in mind that, after a final glance into, the black depths, I nodded to Stark, and we slowly began to descend.

Down, down, down, we made our way step by step, each of us guided by a flashlight. There was no break, turn or irregularity anywhere discernible; the walls above us were smooth as glass, and the ceiling rarely many inches above our heads; the steps were of a uniform depth, width and length, and the angle of our descent remained unvarying. For what purpose had the tunnel been designed? Who had designed it? And when?

Stark, I noticed, was proceeding as if beset with apprehensions; he spoke not a word; his breath came in short, heavy gasps; his manner was groping and cautious, and his eyes staring and questioning as they followed my motions by the rays of the flashlights.

"Come, Andy, let's turn back!" I proposed, after we had gone many hundreds of yards and found no change or new sign of interest.

He stopped short, and peered at me in a doubtful silence, then haltingly requested, "Just a little way further, Dan. This tunnel must lead somewhere."

"Oh, all right..." I grumbled, and as we silently started down once more I felt for my revolver.

Before we had gone another dozen paces, I felt Stark clutching at my arm. "Look!" he exclaimed, sharply. "Look, Dan. See...there ahead of us!"

He had focused the beams of the flashlight in a revealing circle upon a point almost within hand's grasp—and instantly I saw. The wall was covered with markings—deeply engraved markings in a series of jagged, perpendicular lines, similar to those we had observed above ground.

"Well, what do you say to that?" cried Stark, grasping me about the shoulders in quaking agitation.

I stood staring at the hieroglyphics, too astonished to reply. Were the makers of the markings still alive?

However, if they were alive, would it not be perilous to thrust ourselves upon them without formality? So I demanded of Stark, who only laughed at my fears.

"What? Afraid of dead men?" he mocked. "Why, most likely there hasn't been another living thing down here for a million years."

Even as he finished these words, his whole form shuddered convulsively; once more I felt him clutching violently at my arm. "Well, I'll be damned!" he ejaculated, hoarsely, while staring down the passageway like one who has seen a ghost.

"What now?" I demanded, while a wave of dread shot down my spine.

"Look! Down there! Way down there…a light!" he mumbled, pointing into the depths. "I saw it plainly—"

For several seconds I stared in the indicated direction. However, only the deep, unyielding blackness met my eyes.

"Guess your imagination is running away with you?" I commented. "Darkness getting on your nerves. Didn't you say only dead men—"

"Why, there it is…there it is again!" he shrilled, in the same startled manner as before. "I tell you, Dan, I saw it clearly—a low, dim light! It seemed to glide across the aisle—and vanish. Like a lamp carried by a human hand!"

"Strange you saw it and I didn't," I protested, while struggling to keep up my courage. "Come now, I'd swear there's actually nothing there." And then, after a momentary silence, "Well, ready to go back?"

"Go back?" he echoed. "Go back, just when things begin to get interesting? No, Dan, not me. I'm going to see what caused that light. I'd take my oath it was no hallucination."

Although it was my own hope that it was indeed an hallucination, what could I do but agree to accompany Stark?

But not until now had I been conscious of the full terror, the full uncertainty of our adventure. Here we were, two travelers from a far-off world, descending a tunnel of whose purpose or builders we knew nothing; descending into the depths of an unknown planet, perhaps into the very arms of merciless foes. The smooth, sloping stone walls, reaching through the darkness just above our heads and all about us, suddenly struck us as intolerably confining; the still, musty air, permeated with the moldy odors of centuries, seemed dismal and noxious as the air of a prison; the curious acoustics of the tunnel, in which every whisper sounded preternaturally loud and every muttering was magnified into a roar, had a tormenting effect upon our overwrought nerves; while the heavy breathing of my companion as we cautiously stepped down and down, our flashlights wavering through the blackness, served only to accentuate my sense of something heavy bearing down upon us, something ominous, something eerie and foreboding.

I have no idea how long that descent continued; I have only the impression that we covered hundreds of steps without noticing any difference in the straight, sloping vastness of the gallery. All the while, however, I was aware that the air was growing denser and mustier; and that the temperature was rising, until our fur coats were becoming a burden. So profusely, indeed, were we perspiring, and so heavily were we breathing that at last it seemed certain that we would soon have to halt or turn back.

Meanwhile, the lights supposedly seen by Stark did not reappear, I was becoming more and more convinced that they had been mere illusions—when all at once I myself saw something that made me gasp and stop short. It was not exactly a light; rather, it was the suggestion of a light; the blackness ahead of us seemed not quite so black as before, seemed to have been softened to a blank, heavy gray, like that of skies at late twilight. So gradually had the change occurred that I had not noticed how or when it came about.

"Good Lord...what's that?" demanded Stark, who had observed the phenomenon simultaneously. "Surely, there's light ahead!"

"Better not be too sure," I cautioned. "It may vanish— like those other lights you saw."

Stark grinned, and started energetically on his way again. I jogged in his footsteps, still searching and searching the abysses beneath. To my astonishment, the deep gray circle below gradually grew a little less hazy of outline; gradually began to be penetrated by a dull illumination from some mysterious source. And at the same time, adding to our bewilderment, our cheeks were fanned all at once by a faint current of air—faint, but unmistakable, and wonderfully refreshing to our nostrils.

"Where under heaven can that breeze come from—here, hundreds of feet underground?" It was on my lips to ask. However, I kept my thoughts to myself, while my eyes were fascinated by that dim luster ahead of us, a luster gradually expanding into a faint silvery whiteness, with something of a ghostly quality that made it seem like a lantern viewed in a dream.

"Surely, we *are* dreaming!" I told myself; and I bit my lip and prodded my sides to make sure that I was awake. For how, in cold actuality, was it possible to find light here beneath the planet's surface?

"Radioactivity, perhaps. Or else some buried volcanic fire," I was assuring myself—when suddenly, without warning, our tunnel came to an end!

Due to some deceptive arrangement in the faint silvery

light, which presented the illusion of interminable distances still to be covered, we had reached the bottom while we imagined that we were still on the way! Not precisely the bottom, it is true—but the bottom of our own tunnel, which emptied into a greater cavern whose existence we had not previously suspected.

This second gallery, which extended in a horizontal direction as far as our eyes could follow, was the source of the mysterious silvery illumination, which still remained mysterious, since it filled the corridor from no visible luminary. The gallery itself was of the most singular shape imaginable; its sides were patterned on the plan of an equilateral triangle, and the distance from the base to the apex was perhaps twenty feet. As for the floor and walls, they were hewn out of solid granite varied by the peculiar jagged markings we had already observed; while so even were the lines of the corridor, and so exact the proportions, that we murmured in surprise at the engineering skill of the excavators.

From the bottom of our tunnel to the floor of the gallery there was a drop of six or eight feet; but we observed no ladder, stairway or other easy means of descent. The question now arose whether or not to go down to the floor of the main gallery; for while it would be simple enough to climb back if we had the time, we were by no means certain of being able to return in an emergency.

"Well, at least, we have our revolvers," pointed out Stark, tapping significantly at his belt.

"As for me," I suggested, "I prefer to look before I leap."

I do not know what it was that overcame me at that moment; whether it was by the irony of the fates that I lost my footing, or whether the sly hand of Stark helped the fates along. At all events, I do know that, an instant later, I found myself sprawled on the surface of the lower gallery.

Under the plea of coming to my rescue, Stark slipped down beside me, and laughingly diagnosed my worst injury as a skinned knee. However, it seemed to me that there was a tinge of triumphant joy in his tone as he proposed, "Well, Dan, since we're here, suppose we stay? I'm all ready, if you are. Shall we start out to the right—or the left?"

PART TWO

CHAPTER SIX
The Closed Gate

IT WAS ONLY a few minutes before our discoveries began to multiply. The triangular gallery, along whose interminable reaches we had begun to wander, was but one out of many. Other galleries, not triangular in shape, but curved or rectangular, shot out in all directions like side streets from a city's central thoroughfare. Some of these were of smaller proportions; one or two were of equal size or larger; but all alike were cut with mathematical regularity through the solid rock; all were glowing with a faint radiance from some invisible source, and all were deserted as a tomb.

As if these branching corridors were not cause enough for wonder, we came at length into a sort of court, octagonal in shape, and with a ceiling about fifty feet high. Its surprising features were not the smoothness or the evenness of the walls, but rather the designs that decorated them, designs blended in every conceivable hue and shade—a veritable symphony of color! What they represented we could not say; all that we could make out was a confusion of strange, whirling, writhing, sinuous forms, in which creatures half human-shaped were doing a snake-like dance.

Leaving the multi-hued court, we were cautious to advance always in a straight line, lest we lose our way amid the labyrinth. However, we had already gone too far; about a mile or a mile and a half from our point of descent, our gallery abruptly started downward, at an angle of twenty or twenty-five degrees. And Stark, pushing on despite my protest, made two discoveries after going only a few yards: a large metallic screen-like arrangement on the upper walls of the corridor, through which the air was able to flow as through a ventilator; and an enormous opening, five or six feet across, which gaped from the floor of the tunnel, but was likewise covered with a metallic screen.

Curiously the two of us bent down to examine this unexpected device. The metal, which seemed to be some sort of an iron or iron-and-nickel alloy, was fresh-looking and beautifully polished, almost as though placed here only yesterday. Could this appearance be deceptive?

Even as this question flashed through our minds, it was answered from an unlooked-for source.

All at once, we were startled by a loud rattling sound. Only a few yards away, where the gallery began its descent, a heavy sheet of steel, propelled by no visible power, was clattering from its hiding place among the rocks, to cover the tunnel-entrance and cut off our path of retreat. Its movement was not rapid—but, unfortunately, we observed it just a fraction of a second too late; in our terror-stricken dash for the entrance, we had just time to thrust our hands through the closing aperture, and then to withdraw them in haste lest they be crushed.

Now, while we stood staring at one another with drawn white faces, there came a roaring from the screen-covered hole in the floor; a tremendous gust of foul-smelling hot air, like a furnace blast, burst out upon us; and we found ourselves in the midst of a perfect gale of heat and of evil, unimaginable odors, which blew upward from the floor with such violence that we had to struggle to retain our balance.

How furiously we stormed now at the closed gateway. Beating at the unimpressionable metal till our fists were bruised and bloody! Over us both the idea had flashed that our presence had been discovered; that the builders of the galleries, seeing us although unseen by us, had devised a scheme to snare and asphyxiate us. Were we to be doomed like rats in a trap? So we asked, as we stood there clutching and beating at the wall, while over us both there rushed a mad, all-powerful desire for freedom, for fresh air, for the unhampered open spaces.

Possibly our imprisonment lasted only a few minutes, as the clock records time, yet whole worlds of suffering and terror were condensed into that period; a dozen miserable deaths—the concentrated wretchedness of a lifetime! What then was our joy when the roaring in our ears suddenly subsided. When the wind of foul vapors ceased, and we found ourselves once more in silence.

But now appeared a new source of alarm. What were those strange noises, hoarse and gruff, that vibrated from beyond the closed gate? I can best liken them to the grunts of savage beasts, the muttering of enraged grizzlies—even to hear them was to shudder. Yet they did have a variety, a persistency of utterance that was not quite beast-like!

Minute after minute those sounds continued, sometimes barely audible, sometimes rising in a swift booming succession, sometimes dropping to a sort of throaty drawling especially unpleasant to our ears.

"Whatever they are, do you think they know we're inside here?" whispered Stark, in tones almost too low for me to hear. "Shall I give them a reminder?"

"Better not!" I cautioned, feeling for my revolver. However, after a muttered, "Anything's better than being locked here!" my comrade let forth a yell at the top of his voice.

The effect was instantaneous. The sounds from behind the wall rose in a swift, guttural chorus, as though many individuals wished to be heard all at once. There was a series of bellowings and shrill cries, mingled with lower-voiced ejaculations suggestive of surprise; then followed some confused gabblings, and some mutterings so faint that we could scarcely hear them; then all at once, to our consternation, there came a clattering sound, and the metal gate slowly drew open.

We had been prepared for some curious sights, but surely for nothing like this strange reality. Here were not the beasts that the gruff voices had led us to expect! Yet here were creatures only remotely human! Half a dozen shimmering forms, slender as children, but close to seven feet in height, stood before us in rainbow costumes. Their faces, doughy pallid, were each dominated by two enormous bulging greenish eyes; their pole-like arms and legs were naked, their high foreheads were overlooked by pates innocent of hair, their many-jointed fingers were nearly a foot long, and numbered seven on each hand. However, what really distinguished the creatures—what gave them their singular, unearthly appearance, and set them off from humanity—was a glowing phosphorescent orb about three inches across that grew in a socket at the top of the head of each of them: a lantern of flesh and blood, reminding me of the lights of deep-sea fishes!

At the first glimpse, we could merely take in the general features of the strangers. Meanwhile for a moment, they stared back at us without moving, while their greenish, baby-small mouths slid open, their greenish eyes glittered queerly, and the lanterns on their heads flashed more brightly, changing weirdly in hue, till they looked like golden searchlights. Then all at once—almost before we had recovered from our first gasp of surprise—a peculiar babbling arose simultaneously from all the creatures, their lamps took on a lavender tint, and their thin forms rocked back and forth in uncontrollable convulsions. Not until these antics had lasted many seconds; not until the natives began tapping, tapping significantly at their heads, did we realize that they were laughing.

Afterwards, we were to understand that the reason for their laughter was because we had no head-lamps, which made us seem like—to them—how a man with no head at all would seem like to us. But at the time we did not realize this; indeed, we grew indignant to meet with such a reception. And, as a result, we made a serious blunder; we reached into our revolver cases, and brandished our weapons high in air. Neither of us had any intention except to make an impression; but here again chance betrayed us; it was because of my heedless excitement and not by design that my fingers inadvertently pressed the trigger.

The ensuing flash of flame, the smoke, the noise, echoing down the closed corridor like the report of a cannon, had exactly the effect that we might have expected. The Plutonians, after their first terrified screams and yells, one and all whirled about, and, with the agility of antelopes, began racing away along the corridor...until in a moment the last of them, gibbering with fright, had swept out of view.

"Well, now I understand," exclaimed Stark, as the last of the strangers whisked away. "Now I understand those lanterns I saw from the dark stairway. They were the head-lights of passing natives."

Being more interested in safety than in explanations, I attempted no answer, but hastily suggested, "By God, Andy, don't you suppose it's time to be getting out of here? I'm afraid we've made ourselves unpopular enough already with those long-fingered devils."

Stark nodded; and, without a word, we began to retrace our footsteps. Finding the temperature unbearably warm, we stripped off our fur coats, and with these articles dangling from our arms, we pressed on our way as rapidly as our shaken and weary condition would permit.

For a few minutes, our progress was unimpeded. The straight, triangular gallery, with its silvery illumination, stretched out before us silent and untenanted; at last, without incident, we reached the court of the multi-hued decorations, and realized that the stairway to the outer world was not many hundreds of yards off. Then, as we darted forward with cries of relief, an unforeseen obstacle intruded. All at once, the lights went out!

I have no way of picturing the terrorizing suddenness of the effect, I can only say that we were plunged into blackness—blackness absolute and impenetrable. Not the flicker, not the suggestion of a light trembled about us from the thick emptiness; it was as though we had been hurled to the pitchy bottom of the sea.

"Andy! Andy!" I gasped; and, reaching out a swift arm to grasp my friend, I swung it with a crash against the cavern wall. "Andy! Andy!"

At the same time, I heard him just beside me, muttering beneath his breath. "Damn it all!" he mumbled. "Dash those lamp-headed demons—"

Suddenly he broke short. What was that hoarse, throaty noise from somewhere in the darkness?

For a second or two we remained tense and motionless, listening. Then all at once the sound was repeated, nearer and more threatening.

Only now, in our terror, did we remember our flashlights, and fumble for them with uncertain, panic-stricken movements. It was a minute before we could extricate them from amid our clothing; but at length, while Stark was still groping in the gloom, I did find mine.

No sooner had the beams broken the darkness than there came, from just ahead, a shrill, startled cry. I thought I saw a shadowy form that shot across the gallery and vanished; I thought I heard a scampering of swift feet, and made out a yellowish light crazily wavering. But that was all—in less than a second, sights and sounds alike had faded.

"Guess we're safe enough for the time being," muttered Stark, as he also found his flashlight. "Let's go ahead."

Side by side we set out again through the darkness.

However, we little understood the prowess of the enemy. When we had gone only a few yards, we began to be aware of annoying little bands and streamers that entangled our feet and impeded our progress. At first we paid little heed, since the flashlights showed them only as the thinnest little silvery threads, too frail and slender-looking to be worth attention. We did not anticipate how they were to multiply as we advanced, nor how our arms and our whole bodies were to be obstructed, until it was as if our pathway were lined with all, dense brush. Even so, we did not begin to suspect the nature of our antagonist; we did not know the extremity of terror until suddenly, as by one accord, we stumbled, and in falling lost our grip upon the flashlights, which flickered and went out.

Our descent, although precipitate, had not been painful, for we were arrested by something soft and down-like. However, I shall never forget my sensations as I tried to pick myself up again. Now at last I could appreciate the feelings of the deer crushed by the python! I could not rise to my feet! It was as if unseen hands were holding me down; as if unseen arms, yielding, insinuating, irresistible, were winding about my neck, about my shoulders, about my entire form! All that I could feel was those delicate, silken strands; it did not matter how many I evaded or broke; always there were others...others...others; so that the more I struggled, the more I was entangled. By the hundreds, perhaps by the thousands, the tiny threads were around me, caressing me like living things; soon my arms could only squirm convulsively; soon my legs could only kick weakly; soon my whole body,

55

prone on the floor, could only writhe like a fly stuck on the flypaper.

Meanwhile, close at hand, another form threshed and struggled in the darkness.

In my battle with the unseen I had no time for anything except terror. I had no time to reflect on what had happened, to ask whether we could hope for anything better than death… And fortunately, we were spared the ordeal of long waiting. Of a sudden—so unexpectedly that we blinked, and were momentarily blinded—the gallery flashed once more into brightness; and our startled eyes, staring out from amid silvery meshes, made out the forms of several Plutonians gazing down upon us in silent speculation.

For several minutes they remained staring at us without speech or motion, while their head-lights—which evidently had been switched off—were one by one re-illumined. Then at last the leader of the band—a giant, who must have approached eight feet in height—made a peculiar grunting sound, and four of his fellows slid down on the floor beside Stark and myself.

Now suddenly we were to appreciate the advantage of fourteen long, many-jointed fingers. No earthly hands could have worked with the dexterity of the Plutonians; they manipulated like marvelous and infinitely adaptable machines, so swift of action that we could not follow them with our eyes. Almost before we realized it, they had reached among the entanglements of our garments, and removed every detachable article—matches, compass, food, etc., all of which they examined with a curious attention. Then one of them drew forth my revolver, which he threw into a corner, and which immediately discharged, to everyone's loud-voiced terror. Thenceforth the Plutonians handled us with a little more respect; but that did not prevent them from wrapping their long fingers about us and lifting us bodily into a three-wheeled canoe-shaped cart; after which, with the silvery meshes wound about us so tightly that we had trouble to breathe, we were rolled away amid a gibbering escort.

Within a few minutes, we reached the end of a low, short gallery, from which a black hole about five feet across shot off into vacancy. Regardless of our howling protest, our cart was shoved toward this opening and slowly forced through it. Naturally we twisted and struggled as furiously as our bound condition would permit; we fancied we could read the mutterings of a malevolent glee in the excited speech of our captors, and had visions of being flung into some dark tremendous chasm. Yet our protests were like those of a child caught in an avalanche. Down into the darkness we were pushed deliberately, remorselessly; we heard a door clatter shut behind us; the throaty speech of the Plutonians grew faint in our ears, and there was a grinding of wheels and a roaring as we went whirling away through interminable spaces.

In a torrent the wind rushed past us while our car traveled, perhaps on rails, around long curves and windings. At first, in our bewilderment, it did not occur to us that the motive-power was gravity; that the curves and grades of the tunnel had been calculated with mathematical precision; that we had been consigned to some particular destination, as certainly as a letter sent through a mail tube. However, it was with intense relief that, after many minutes of traveling, we finally felt our headlong speed relaxing; felt the car moving more and more slowly, like an automobile coasting to a stop, until it halted with a jerk as though it had struck some solid barrier.

For a moment the darkness was still impenetrable... Then, of a sudden, there came a blinding brilliance, a gate flashed open before us, and we heard a tumult of heavy voices. And immediately we were surrounded by loud-mouthed bands of

Plutonians, and carried out into a place of unimaginable weirdness and beauty.

Nothing we had seen in the galleries above could have led us to expect this gigantic corridor, this world beneath a world, which darted before our astonished view. At the first glimpse, we could only gaze and gasp, and only by degrees did the full features of this buried universe begin to make themselves plain.

Picture a cavern large enough to contain a city; a cavern with an arching, vaguely illuminated rocky roof five hundred feet high; a cavern a thousand feet across, and longer than the unaided eye can measure. Picture the walls patterned of fifty blending pastel shades, all of them ever-changing from some invisible source of radiance; picture niches containing intricate and tremendous carved figures, which likewise shift in color as though played upon by unseen lanterns; picture the whole vast gallery supported by no columns and yet shaped into a series of cyclopean domes, each fashioned with such precision and symmetry that you could stare and marvel never-endingly.

However, in the beginning, Stark and I had little chance to stare and marvel. Awe inspiring as was the cavern, our attention was fastened more closely upon the mob that surrounded us.

At first we could see that many of these people were unlike any we had thus far observed. All were distinguished by lamps growing at the tops of their heads and frequently changing color, from purple to vermilion, from vermilion to golden, from golden to violet, all had features pale as dough and great bulging greenish eyes; and all were fourteen-fingered, and so slender as to remind me of walking reeds. However, aside from this, they manifested a great variety. Their height ranged from three feet to eight, while the size of their heads was subject to a great diversity. Here and there strode an individual with a head four times larger than the average. But even more striking was the difference in their costumes. Some wore shimmering multi-hued garments such as we had first seen, others displayed diaphanous white robes transparent as gauze, and still others, including most of the big-headed species, had dispensed entirely with artificial encumbrances, and walked in unembarrassed nakedness.

Upon our arrival, Stark and I were lifted out of the car by half a dozen of the tallest natives and carried to an elevated stone platform, about whose base the lamp-heads had gathered in a vociferous concourse. Then, greatly to our relief, the strands that bound us were untied, and we had the pleasure of being able to stand once more on our feet. Surrounded by a guard that precluded any attempt at escape, we were allowed to flex and unbend our stiffened muscles, and meanwhile we noticed how agreeably warm was the atmosphere, and fresh and sweet.

During the brief delay, while we were exercising and rubbing our arms and legs and restoring the circulation, I noticed that our fur coats lay spread on the floor of the platform, and that two lamp-heads were examining them through microscope-like tubes with the most ridiculous gravity. They would pass the lenses over each bit of the surface in turn, squint their green eyes, and allow their head-lamps to revolve in all directions; and after each stage of the inspection they would turn to one another, nod in a puzzled manner, utter an unintelligible phrase or two, hold a hair or patch of hairs to the light, and then return to the examination.

Meanwhile the members of the mob below were pointing to us excitedly; gibbering; and significantly tapping their heads; while from time to time we heard babbling explosions of laughter. It was only too evident that they regarded us as some sort of a circus exhibition.

What was more, they had not long to wait for the

performance to begin. After a few minutes one of the great-headed type, whose upper extremity seemed vastly too big for his slender shoulders, edged his way out of the multitude, which cleared a path respectfully before him. He was by far the largest we had yet seen, and towered to a height well above eight feet. Like many of his brainy-looking brethren, he wore no clothes; yet we were puzzled as to the sex of the creature; I can only say that the pallid stick of a body was hairless and unprepossessing, and displayed the charms neither of Apollo nor of Venus.

None the less, it seemed that he was a person of distinction; upon his arrival on the platform, a silence fell across the assemblage, and all stood waiting with their greenish eyes blazing and their tiny open mouths upturned in expectation.

Placing himself cautiously near to a stairway about ten feet to our right, he launched into a series of grunts, hoots and mumblings evidently addressed to us. Every few seconds he would pause, stare at us as if he expected a reply, and then proceed with a different intonation, but although he must have made fifty or sixty tries, the results were always the same. Long before he had finished, the changes in his manner and accentuation had made it clear that he was a linguist testing us in various languages.

Finally, after exhausting his repertory, he seemed to come to the conclusion that we were either unfathomably stupid, or else deaf and dumb. For he lifted his fourteen long fingers, and manipulated them as if motioning in sign language; while the eager look in his jade-like eyes showed plainly that he expected a response.

Our patience having been exhausted, Stark and I both opened our mouths at once to speak.

"Come, we're not dummies!" he exclaimed, forgetting that the Plutonians did not understand English. "No need to talk that way—" I started to protest…when hundreds of babbling voices broke out in a contagion of laughter that cut us rudely short.

Even our interlocutor could not resist the general uproar; for several minutes he rocked back and forth in gusty mirth.

However, after the tumult had subsided, he seemed to feel that the examination had gone far enough. Without further delay he motioned to a group of shimmering-gowned individuals, who mounted the platform, formed themselves about Stark and me in the manner of a military escort, and marched us away into the depths of the vast vaulted gallery.

CHAPTER SEVEN
In the Hands of the Lamp-Heads

IT WAS a long and tortuous journey that we made in the company of our rainbow-robed escort—a journey so strange and unexpected that Stark and I could only stare at the passing scenes in unbelieving confusion. Part of the distance we covered on foot, but the greater percentage was managed by means of a moving iron platform, which whirled us across space with the velocity of an express train. We went shooting through long, unlighted tunnels; we came out into high-roofed, brilliantly lighted caverns, featured by some grayish fungus-like vegetation; we caught sight of huge revolving steely machines with wheels as wide as a city block; we had a glimpse of an underground river or canal, whose waters rushed in a torrential, straight-banked course; and everywhere we saw swarms of natives, always distinguished by their head-lamps, and always of the same slender, stringy build.

Finally our platform came to a halt in a many-branching gallery, whose tall fretted roof reminded me of some gorgeous cathedral. We were then conducted on foot along one of the innumerable passageways, meanwhile observing that the pavement was of some yielding, rubber-like substance, and that long triangular openings, evidently doors, were placed at frequent intervals. However, we did not recognize this as a residential section, until at last we were ushered through one of the doors into a series of enormous rooms with arching ceilings and windowless, tapestry-covered walls. The light, we noticed, was mellow and even, and transfused the apartments from some invisible source; the air, likewise, was blowing in a current we knew not whence; the furniture was of the simplest, and consisted only of some marble chests on which our hosts squatted cross-legged, in Oriental fashion; while the floors were multi-colored mosaics apparently commemorating some fabulous events.

Upon entering these rooms, Stark and I had one of the greatest shocks of our lives. Suddenly our ears were assaulted by the most terrific bellowing we had ever heard; and a lanky black monster, big as a colt, and with six great sprawling legs, leapt out of an inner chamber. His cavernous greenish mouth, set with spiky teeth, opened like a crocodile's; a yellowish foam played about his curling lips; his long, donkey-like ears stood erect; a red lamp glowed on his head; and his little red eyes glared with a malicious fire. With a lithe jump he was upon us; his foul breath was hot upon my cheeks; his howling dinned in my ears; I felt one of his great paws upon my breast as he reared upon his hind legs. In that terrified instant I was ready to give myself up for lost; I shrank against the walls, and screamed in dread; nor did I notice the laughter of the lamp-heads. I only know that I did not feel the expected tearing claws; the Plutonians uttered something sharp and rattling, and the beast instantly turned toward one of our guides.

To my amazement, the Plutonian stroked the black hairless skin affectionately, and even received and fondled one of the terrible hooked paws. And the beast opened its ferocious-looking mouth in a yawn, and uttered a sound like a low contented purr.

After our introduction to the Plutonian dog—as Stark and I named the brute, although it might equally well have been called the Plutonian tiger—the lamp-heads motioned us to squat upon one of the chests. This we did after a little hesitation, although not without an uncomfortable longing for chairs. Several of our escorts now retired, but in a moment returned, bearing metal vessels containing water and various suspicious-smelling pasty substances, which they placed before us expectantly. It was as if they had read our thoughts, for we were both hungry and thirsty; but while we accepted the water gratefully, we regarded the pasty concoction with long hesitation. All were most unappetizing to our nostrils as well as to our eyes; the most pleasant-looking reminded me of a form of blue glue, while the others ranged in appearance from moldy flour to stewed sawdust. In addition, there were a few small white capsules, which the gestures of our hosts particularly urged us to try, but which we avoided in favor of the other articles.

Observing no knives, forks or spoons, we were about to plunge in with our fingers, when we were dissuaded by the laughter of our new friends, who pointed gleefully to long tubes sticking from the vessels and made significant sucking motions. Accordingly, we each doubtfully applied our lips to one of the tubes. The result, I am sorry to say, was not to our liking; Stark's wry face was certainly matched by my own; our mouths were filled with a taste as of stale mush. Besides, there was a certain peculiar, vaguely chemical taste that added to our repugnance; had we not been almost famished, we would surely not have partaken.

However, it would be ungrateful to speak ill of our hosts, who, as I later learned, had offered us of their best. And I should not say anything unkindly about the ordeal that followed, which doubtless also was intended for our good— the ordeal of making us into imitation Plutonians, by the simple method of a change in dress. Without so much as giving us warning or asking our leave, several of the lamp-heads began to fumble about among our clothes; and almost before we were aware what was happening, we stood half disrobed. Apparently not understanding the principles of earthly apparel, they had ripped off the buttons in the act of removing each garment; but we found it useless to resist their marvelously dexterous seven-fingered hands, which seemed capable of ten motions while we were performing one. At last, despite our protests, we were wholly naked; and as we huddled before them in embarrassment, we had to submit to having our bodies examined in detail, while repeated exclamations of wonder or surprise arose from the gathering as each new wart, tuft of hair or carbuncle was inspected. Our beards and moustaches were particularly the subjects of attention, and were scrutinized and pulled again and again in a manner to evoke our loud resentment. Worst of all, just as the investigation began, we were joined by one of those top-heavy Plutonians with the extra-sized heads who led in the inspection, and, after each new finding, turned to a small white object that we took for a notebook, and excitedly jotted down a few words.

For some time, even after the examination was over, it seemed doubtful whether we would be given clothes at all. While we stood shivering, a heated debate arose, in which everyone except Stark and I participated, and which the six-legged beast punctuated with occasional howls. But in the end, fortunately, the pro-clothes party emerged victorious; the hubbub died down, and two of the lamp-heads vanished, to return almost immediately with some shimmering, multi-hued costumes, such as we had observed on many Plutonians.

Now began a battle royal. It was as if they had tried to fit a wild boar into the skin of a gazelle; both Stark and I, while tall and fairly slender as men go on Earth, were much too short and vastly too stout for the sinuous Plutonian garments. Even though the clothes were made of some rubbery substance, our limbs would not adjust themselves to their outlandish proportions; nor would their proportions adjust themselves to our limbs. The result was that our new apparel split in many places, leaving strips of our skin exposed; but this did not deter our persecutors, who ended by slicing off a foot or two of the costumes, leaving us in possession of the rest, splits and all. For footgear we were then presented with slender straw-like sandals; and thus, arrayed in the native fashion, with bursting clothes that shone and shimmered as we walked, we made a spectacle that our friends on Earth would have found it hard to recognize.

It may be imagined that, after the unusual hardships of the day, Stark and I were weary to the point of exhaustion. But once again, fortunately, the Plutonians seemed almost to have read our thoughts. After spreading mats and pillows of some bamboo-like substance across two of the chests, they motioned us to lie down; and when we had complied, they mumbled something unintelligible, and, accompanied by the bellowing beast, retreated from the room.

At the same time, with welcome suddenness, the lights went out. The darkness was now absolute, the silence complete; and in another moment Stark and I, forgetting the scenes and adventures of the day, had left Pluto worlds behind us in dreams of a planet where men wore no lamps on their heads but laughed in the heartening light of the sun.

PART THREE

CHAPTER EIGHT
Enter the Third Sex

I SHALL NOT linger over the monotonous days and weeks that followed. Stark and I were prisoners, although prisoners treated without severity; we were confined within a series of connecting rooms and corridors that seemed to comprise a small world within themselves; we were forced to devote our attention, during the greater part of our waking hours, to a study that proved fascinating even if irksome, but that we knew to be of the utmost importance. In a word, we were being taught Plutonian. Each day—or each period of about twenty hours, which constituted the native unit of time—several tutors would take turns for hours in giving us an elementary education. Their method in the beginning, of course, was wholly by means of signs; they would perform various actions, or would point to various objects and the various parts of their bodies and make appropriate sounds, after which they would scribble the corresponding symbols on bits of parchment-like paper—and we would be required to repeat the performance after them, both as to the writing and the speaking.

Evidently, though, we did not make good pupils. From their disgusted gestures, I know that they regarded our progress as discouragingly slow. I writhe even in memory to think of their disdainful grimaces upon hearing our efforts to imitate their thick-mouthed speech; and I clench my fists in involuntary anger when I recall their condescending manner at our attempts to string sentences together grammatically.

"Grangrum! Grangrum!" they would repeatedly mutter to themselves—an expression which I later learned to be the equivalent of our "Jackass."

Nevertheless, when I remember the difficulties of their speech, which put verbs first, nouns second, and adverbs, adjectives and prepositions last, I believe that both Stark and I made remarkable progress and did very well in being able, within a few weeks, to combine words and phrases in an understandable if not a grammatical order, and so to hold our first conversations.

It was only natural, of course, that our minds should be swarming with questions to put to the Plutonians; but it had hardly occurred to us that they might have an equal number of questions to put to us, and that they had perhaps educated us for this very reason. At all events, when they finally saw that we were capable of exchanging ideas, a most interesting colloquy ensued.

Not less than eight or ten distinguished-looking Plutonians had been summoned for the occasion. All were of the huge-headed variety, with brilliant top-lamps constantly changing in color, and with little or no clothing; and all carried pads of the parchment-like paper, upon which they wrote volumi-nously. Not until long afterwards did we learn how we were being honored—for that delegation, though we did not suspect it, included the planet's foremost anthropologist, a representative of its most influential newspaper, one of the heads of the Plutonian international state, and two of the world's leading zoologists.

After the party had arrived to the tune of a weird music wafted from some unseen radio, they all seated themselves cross-legged on mat-covered chests; and the most imposing-looking of them all—he who, we later learned, was a prominent statesman—soberly began the interview.

We could not catch more than half of his opening words,

though I do know that his fellow investigators looked interested and applauded abundantly. We did, however, make out the drift of his concluding sentences, which were to the effect that our arrival had created a worldwide consternation, and that there were several theories as to our origin, none of which had been finally accepted.

"So now we want you to decide for us," he ended, speaking slowly and deliberately, and picking only the simplest words, as a grown man might do when addressing a four-year-old. "Tell us, where is it that you come from?"

All the lamp-heads leaned forward breathlessly; there was a moment of tense silence before Stark replied:

"It is as you have probably guessed. We do not come from this world. We come from far away in outer space."

A chorus of excited ejaculations filled the room. "Not from this world? From far away? From outer space? By my lamp, what does he mean? Preposterous! Preposterous!"

Our interlocutor, the renowned statesman, alone preserved an unruffled gravity.

"Comrades, do not be disturbed," he counseled, lifting seven reassuring fingers. "This is just as I have suspected. We all know, of course, that there is no such thing as another world—the very idea is absurd. But what our friend means is that he comes from deep down in this world."

"No," exclaimed Stark, "that is not what I mean!"

Disregarding this outburst, the Plutonian continued, "Now you know, comrades, that not all the world has been explored. Far, far down, where the heat grows great, and where all things become lighter and fall but slowly, we have not dug our galleries. But there are legends that galleries have been dug even there by barbarian races, unlike our own. Perhaps some of these aborigines—" here he pointed significantly to his head—"have not advanced to our own high stage. Perhaps some of them are even lacking in the most important of human organs, the lamp. Now is it not possible that such unfortunates, if they exist, should from time to time send up scouts to explore the civilized lands?"

The speaker ended impressively, and the other lamp-heads nodded agreement.

Of course Stark and I tried our best to convince them of their error. We assured them, as well as we were able, that we had not come from anywhere on their own planet; that we had originated on a world so far away that it would take light several hours to cover the distance. With our limited knowledge of the native language—which seemed to have no words for "planet," "Earth," or "sun"—we had great difficulty in making our ideas plain; in fact, the greater part of what we said passed completely over the people's heads. They did, however, understand our references to the speed of light, and the time it would take to travel from our own world—and their thin, pasty faces, at this information, were twisted into comical smirks, which soon gave way to babbling laughter.

When their merriment had subsided, one of them—whom I later came to know as a famous scientist—screwed his tiny mouth into an expression of ludicrous gravity, and stared at us reprovingly with his great greenish eyes.

"I would have you understand," he growled, "that we are serious investigators, who will stand for no flippancy. The truth, and the truth alone, is what we want. Now everyone knows that, at the distance that you mention, there is nothing at all. Only blackness, and empty air, or else dead rock, without tunnels or galleries. We have never been able to decide which, although tradition says that far above our galleries there are open spaces, from which our ancestors retreated ages ago. However, that was before history began, and the old legends have never been confirmed. We only know that no one, within remembered times, has been able to venture more than a certain distance upward without perishing in the cold. And yet you mean to tell us that you come from a million, a hundred million times as far?"

New spasms of laughter racked the investigators. It was minutes before they were able to relax into seriousness; and when they did so it was our turn to attempt a questionnaire. We asked what they knew as to the sun, the stars and the planets, but found that, as we already suspected, the heavenly bodies were not only unknown but inconceivable to them. There was indeed an ancient myth as to the existence of such luminaries, but no one now regarded it as anything more than a fabrication of the childhood of the race. In the beginning, from all that we could make out, the Plutonians had lived on their planet's surface, but had been driven underground long ago, when the growing cold had threatened them with extermination—so long ago that the recollection hardly existed now even as a racial memory.

Although there were a thousand questions that Stark and I wished to ask as to life underground, we had to restrain our impatience while we listened to views and queries regarding ourselves. What particularly interested the members of the committee was our lack of top-lamps; they regarded our light-less heads with an irritating sympathy, and seemed to look upon us as we would look upon the blind; while one of them went so far as to ask how we managed to find our way in dark places, to read in the dark, or to enjoy life generally without these appendages. "Besides," he added, in the most incomprehensible manner, while his head-lamp glowed from violet to a deep purple, "how do you convey your feelings?"

We both stared at him in confusion. "Why, what of our tongues?" Stark at length managed to sputter.

Immediate laughter was his response.

"Your tongues may possibly convey your thoughts," conceded our interviewer, after his mirth had subsided. "But how about the real essence of your life, your emotions?"

"What have head-lamps to do with emotions?" demanded Stark.

A fresh babbling of laughter echoed throughout the room. Some of the Plutonians, it seemed to us, nodded to one another as you might nod when a child asks some impossible question.

However, upon being persuaded that we actually did not know what they were laughing about, one of the scientists went on to report:

"Well, among our people, you see, head-lamps are the most valuable registers of emotions. They are flawlessly accurate, because we cannot control them except by covering them or deliberately letting them go out. Each subtle shade of feeling is represented by a different tint or color in the head-lamp; and there are so many tints and colors that I cannot begin to mention them all. Thus, if one of us is a little frightened, his head-lamp will turn a faint yellow. If he is more frightened, it will become a brighter yellow; if he is terrorized, it will glow to a brilliant yellow. Again, if he is annoyed or irritated, it will take on a pink shade; if he becomes slightly angry, it will turn light—red, if he is enraged, it will leap to a vivid scarlet. And so with all the other colors. Each expresses a particular emotion, and there is no emotion that they cannot indicate. It is therefore impossible for any of us to conceal our feelings while our lamps are burning; you have only to glance at a neighbor's head to know what is going on in his heart."

"So you see," added another Plutonian, while he felt caressingly for his own luminary, "so you see what you miss by not possessing a lamp!"

I smiled in acknowledgment, yet reflected that I was not missing a great deal in being able to keep my feelings to myself.

The Plutonians, however, were still profuse in their expressions of sympathy; and even suggested that, since we could not indicate our feelings by means of head-lamps, we had no feelings to indicate at all.

After commenting unfavorably on our red lips and five-fingered hands, the investigators turned their attention to our beards and hair, which they examined with solemn interest, inquiring how it came to be there and whether it was natural or had been planted. Their original impression was that it was a species of vegetation sown by means of spores or seeds; and only after the most exasperating argumentation could we relieve them of this idea. Even so, some of them could not be convinced, for nothing like hair, they assured us, had ever been known to their people; the nearest thing to it in appearance was a certain grass-like weed which they grew to feed their domestic animals.

We were relieved when the Plutonians turned to another subject. "What is your age?" they inquired, while several of them bent expectantly over their notebooks.

Since the gauge of Plutonian time is not the same as our own, we had to ponder before replying. Their year is equal to several of our centuries, and the common measurement of time is the sequon, which consists of five hundred twenty-hour days, and is therefore equal to a little less than fourteen months. Accordingly, it appeared that Stark and I, who were approaching our twenty-ninth year, were each about twenty-four sequons of age.

This fact we conveyed to our interviewer as soon as we had performed the necessary process of mental arithmetic. Little, though, did we expect the result.

"Twenty-four sequons!" they all exclaimed, in chorus.

"Impossible!" And their head-lamps blazed to an orange that, we afterwards learned, was indicative of astonishment. "Impossible?" Stark and I echoed in one voice, wondering if we had represented ourselves as Methuselahs. "Why, most of our people live much longer than that."

A babbling of laughter, accompanied by lavender lights of amusement, was our only response.

"Why should you doubt us?" protested Stark, a little indignantly. "Is twenty-four sequons so very long to live?"

Renewed laughter greeted this outburst.

"My friends, you have a peculiar humor," stated one of the Plutonians as, regaining his gravity, he soberly addressed us. "But humor is out of place. We are looking for facts. Of course, you are more than twenty-four sequons of age, for despite your puerile ideas, you are plainly not children. Since the accepted age of maturity is fifty-four sequons—"

"Fifty-four sequons!" muttered Stark. And then to me, on the side, "Good Lord, that's more than sixty years!"

"As the accepted age of maturity is fifty-four sequons," proceeded the Plutonian, a little annoyed at the interruption, "we must recognize that as your minimum age. Most likely you are three or four times as old. This stands to reason, since persons of less than a hundred or a hundred and fifty sequons are hardly to be regarded as having completed their education, much less as being released for the duties of adult life. From that age until six or eight hundred—"

"By the sacred gods..." I burst out, unable to hold back these words in English. "Do you suppose we're older than Christopher Columbus?" And then, checking myself and returning to the Plutonian speech, "Tell me, how old do people here get to be?"

The Plutonian stroked his hairless face with seven meditative fingers. "Well, not so old as we should like—not by any means—though science, of recent ages, has added scores of sequons to our lives. The average person, I am sorry to say, does not live to be more than nine hundred or a thousand. Only in a few unusual cases have fifteen hundred or two thousand been recorded—"

"Two thousand…more than two thousand years!" I gasped, reverting again to English in my excitement.

"How old do your own people get to be?" asked one of the Plutonians, noting our amazement.

We informed him that sixty or seventy sequons marked the usual limit—a statement which, I fear, was taken just a little skeptically.

"Sixty or seventy sequons?" cried one of our hearers. "Why, that is barbarism…a criminal waste. To throw your lives away in the very bud. Is your science then so undeveloped that it cannot repair waste tissues, replace worn out organs, and renew the human frame for even a few hundred sequons?"

Being forced to admit the charges, we were informed how, by a process of creative surgery, the Plutonians were able to remove every part of the body as soon as it showed signs of decay and supplant it with new tissues developed in the laboratory. Thus, in the course of thousands of sequons, the average life had been lengthened tenfold. When at last, to our relief, the Plutonians had abandoned the question of our age, they turned to an even more embarrassing subject.

"Which of the three sexes do you belong to?" one of them startled us by asking.

"Three sexes?" we gasped, uncomprehendingly.

"Three sexes, of course. Which are you—male, female, or Neuter?"

"Why, what—what do you mean by Neuter?" demanded Stark.

The orange hue of surprise was apparent on the head-lamps of all the company.

"By Neuter," explained one of our visitors, shaking his head as if to say that we were really quite impossible, "by Neuter we mean just what we say. We mean, of course, neither male nor female. Look at me—" here he pointed to his long, unclothed body— "it is my pride to be a Neuter myself. And so, I need hardly add, are most of our other distinguished guests."

"Then a Neuter really has no sex?" inquired Stark, as a smile of faint comprehension shot across his face, "He has nothing to do with—with racial perpetuation?"

"Not with physical perpetuation—not at all," declared the Plutonian, whose lamp still showed an orange tint. "There are others whose place it is to attend to such menial duties. But we Neuters have everything to do with the mental perpetuation of the race. We are the transmitters of the arts and sciences, of poetry, music and philosophy. It is we who hand down everything that makes it worth while for the race to continue."

"Then you are a sort of superior caste?" I suggested. "An hereditary class—"

"No, not hereditary. We are Neuters mainly by our own choice. Birth has nothing to do with our high estate."

I am afraid that Stark and I both wore the expression of a blank wall. We did not know whether to believe the speaker; we did not know what to reply; we could only assure him, in halting syllables, that no triple division of the sexes was known among our own people.

Perceiving that our statements were sincere, the Plutonians expressed their surprise by means of orange flashes; and one of them, after a suitable interval, made bold to explain:

"Ages ago, our race also had only two sexes. Every individual—the sages, the artists, the leaders of the State, no less than the lowly—had then to take part in child-bearing or rearing, and to waste many sequons under the proddings of passion or in the fruitless pursuit of love. However, even at the dawn of civilization, we were able to perceive how irrational all this was. Could not the physical needs of the race be served by the commonplace majority, leaving the distinguished few to pursue their studies without distraction? Long investigation and research had proved that genius or even exceptional talent was rarely inherited; hence there could be no racial loss were the individuals of ability to escape the slavery of the sexes. How to effect their release was of course the problem; it was only after ten thousand sequons that the great Darevi, one of the ablest scientists known to history, devised a scheme whereby any male or female could voluntarily transform himself into a Neuter, diverting the sexual energy into channels conducive to the vast enlargement of the cranial cavity and accordingly of the brain. I shall not describe the means whereby the change was brought about, except to say that it operated through a transfusion of the glandular energy, and involved a series of minute and delicate surgical incisions resulting in pronounced organic changes. However, the plan has worked beneficently for scores of thousands of sequons, and today any male or female who, upon approaching maturity, is adjudged to show sufficient promise, is privileged to undergo the necessary treatment and pursue the consecrated career of a Neuter."

"You mean, then, that they must pursue that career?" inquired Stark, "or merely that they may?"

"They may—there is no compulsion in the matter of a lifework. However, it is considered an honor and an opportunity to be adjudged worthy of Neuterhood, and few are willing to let the chance go by. Of course, the chosen ones are allowed a little time—usually ten or twelve sequons—in which to make up their minds. However, once the choice has been made, it is unalterable."

Following this explanation, a long silence fell, and it seemed that the meeting was about to break up. The lamp-heads were already picking up their notebooks, and several were rising from their squatting positions on the mat-covered chests.

None the less, it occurred to Stark to put another query.

"If you don't mind," he began, rather haltingly. "If you don't mind, I wonder if you wouldn't tell me why so many of you Neuters go about without clothes?"

Lavender lights of amusement again appeared in all corners of the room.

"What a ridiculous question," returned one of the lamp-heads. "Why should we need clothes? The air down here is warm; we will not freeze, and not being either males or females, we do not require garments for the sake of sexual allurement or concealment. Besides, are not the robes that nature gave us more handsome than anything we can make? It is true, here and there you do find a radical Neuter who prefers a man-made skin; but this usually occurs only when he has some bodily defect to hide."

By this time most of the lamp-heads had gathered up their books, and some were already drifting out of the room. That, however, did not deter us from a final question—what was to be our lot after we had finished our education in the native language?

It seemed to Stark and me that there was a strange hesitation about the reply. Several minutes passed in silence, while the lamps of all our visitors grew dull and murky and burnt with a sooty flame. We were still too inexperienced to know what this might mean; but our suspicions were not relieved when one of our interviewers assured us:

"Have no fear, my friends. Wait and find out. Trust us— we are arranging everything for your own good. Have no fear at all."

"Have no fear at all..." echoed the others, while their lamps grew even duller of hue and threatened to go out. "No, no, you need have no fear at all."

I do not know why, but something in that repeated phrase

aroused our alarm, I glanced at Stark in apprehension, and he glanced back at me with a perplexed and worried look; and then both of us, with unconcealed misgivings, let our eyes follow the Plutonians as the last of them vanished from the room. Their head-lamps, we noticed, were flickering and failing, and several were already quenched to a lifeless black.

CHAPTER NINE
Zandaye

DURING the weeks that followed, our education continued, monotonously, uneventfully. Gradually we were gaining skill in the native speech; gradually we were learning to read the native books, which, with their jagged script that reached down Chinese-fashion from the top of the page, were the most difficult of all our problems to master. But how well they repaid our efforts! Even the elementary textbooks, designed for small children, solved a thousand mysteries. Thus we earned something about the Plutonian government, a democracy whose head was chosen by means of competitive examination held every ten sequons among selected Neuters. We discovered, at the same time, that there was only one government for the entire planet; and that it had ruled continuously, disturbed by no uprising, for more than a hundred thousand sequons. More important still, we were enlightened regarding the scientific management of Pluto—for only by virtue of their scientific attainments had the Plutonians survived for ages in their unnatural environment.

I shall not attempt to go into detail, particularly since I shall return to some phases of the subject. I need only say that the secret of the success of the lamp-heads was to be found in radioactivity; they were fortunate enough to possess apparently inexhaustible supplies of the radioactive metals, and thanks to this abundant energy they heated the tremendous corridors and caverns that had been bored throughout the ages. They converted the power of radium into electricity, and lighted their galleries by means of tubes concealed just beneath the surface in order to avoid needless glare; they employed the radioactive forces to excavate the corridors and to empty the byproducts of the excavations into enormous subterranean fissures (probably the vents of extinct volcanoes). However, most important of all was the use of radium in industry, and particularly in the state-owned "oxygen industry." For it was necessary for the Plutonians to disintegrate various oxides constantly if they would keep the underground atmosphere fresh and pure. Correspondingly, it was important to relieve themselves of the used or polluted air; and this they accomplished through gigantic pumps, which at stated intervals would discharge the foul air into the upper corridors by means of vents constructed ages ago, Stark and I now realized that, shortly after our arrival upon the planet, it had been our misfortune to be caught in one of these vents just as the waste air was being pumped through; and this explained the sudden closing of the gates, which had trapped us so unexpectedly.

Another question answered by the books was one that had puzzled us for weeks—that of the food supply. The chemistry of foods, we learned, had been studied on Pluto to an extent not remotely approached on earth; the process had extended not only to analysis but to synthesis, and the great bulk of the planet's food supply was manufactured in the laboratory. Virtually all starches and sugars were produced under the influence of a sun-like illumination upon carbon and water; fats and oils were made by a more intricate process, whose formula I was never able to discover; while proteins alone remained beyond the power of scientists to imitate, and had to be extracted from plants grown in great caverns under the stimulation of a sort of artificial sunlight. Yet the flesh of animals—the chief source of proteins on earth—appeared to be unknown as an article of diet.

Since not more than five per cent of the planet's food came from vegetables, there was a natural deficiency in certain organic salts and acids. Hence these too were produced in the laboratory, and were consumed at each meal in the form of small white capsules—which explains the pills that the lamp-heads had urged us to swallow along with our first meal. As for the various pasty, mush-like foods taken through tubes—these were synthetic products that constituted the worldwide staple and were consumed day after day, year after year without change or variety by the five thousand million inhabitants of the planet. The idea that food might be taken for pleasure was a notion that seems never to have penetrated the Plutonian intellect; the lamp-heads regarded eating from the most coldly practical point of view, as a necessary evil; they ate just as they breathed, only in order that they might not die, and expected no more enjoyment than from the circulation of their blood or the functioning of their kidneys. Hence nothing seemed more natural to them than to live upon capsules and mush.

To Stark and myself, however, this diet did not seem inevitable. Neither of us had ever been known as epicures; indeed, we had not complained at having to confine ourselves to dried and canned goods during our long flight on the *Wanderer of the Skies*; but there were limits even to our endurance. Oh, how we longed now for a good old homely plate of beans! How our mouths watered at the thought of corned beef and cabbage! What fortunes we would have given for a dish of ham and eggs! However, it would have been as sensible to ask for the sunlight itself as for these delicacies of the dead past. Nothing half so good; nothing even one hundredth part so good was to be had even by the most fortunate Plutonian; and the worst of it was that the natives merely stared blankly, without a glint of understanding, when we suggested a change in our bill of fare.

However, even the most tractable nature, when sorely tried, will finally rise in revolt. Our longing for culinary variety was to cause us no end of trouble—as matters gastronomical have caused our kind for ages past. Before I describe that event, though, let me report one or two other happenings.

As our education advanced, we had any number of tutors, most of them indistinguishable one from the other, for most of them acted as though we were machines to be operated by switches and levers. However, there was one who differed from all the rest. Shorter in build than most of her fellows, this individual (who went by the name of Zandaye) did not reach above the level of our shoulders, and at the same time was not nearly so slender as most Plutonians. Her proportions—I say "her," since she timidly confessed to being neither a male nor a Neuter—were those of the most sylph-like woman; her eyes, which did not bulge like the eyes of her sisters, were not green but blue; her lips, likewise, were not green but red-tinged, so that altogether—had it not been for her head-lamp and her seven-fingered hands—we might almost have imagined her one of our own people.

Little did we realize at first how these advantages were regarded by her kin. For, when we congratulated her upon her form and the color of her eyes, she seemed almost ready for tears; her voice trembled, her head-lamp turned red, and she appeared to believe herself the butt of our jokes. It was only after long insistence that we learned the reason for her queer behavior. She was regarded as a sort of freak; that her reddish lips were held to be unnatural; that her blue eyes were considered a mark of atavism, of degeneracy, since most of the lower animals on Pluto also had blue eyes; while her perfectly proportioned form was condemned as ludicrously obese.

We assured Zandaye that she did not seem monstrously heavy to us, but she went on to say that her weight—which, translated into our scale of measurements, would be about a hundred pounds—was double the normal maximum for her height. "However," she added—and now her face brightened, and her head-lamp took on the loveliest golden hue—" that does not keep me from advancing intellectually. Out of a class of more than a hundred last sequon, I was one of eleven judged worthy to become a Neuter."

"A Neuter?" I exclaimed, as much shocked as if she had said that she was to enter a nunnery. "Certainly, you're not going to let yourself be thrown away like that?"

"But by my lamp it is not to be thrown away," she flashed back. "It is to be consecrated. To be sure, I still have a few sequons left to decide—but, after all, what is there to decide? I will not be one of those who prefer a career of love—who would ever love a misshapen creature like me?"

Seeing Zandaye standing before us with a piteous, forlorn expression in her great blue eyes, Stark and I were almost ready to forget her head-lamp and her fourteen long fingers. At least, I know that a confession was trembling on my lips, and I fear that Stark was half-ready to blot out the thought of a certain black-haired temptress several billions of miles away.

But although we still did not let our emotions master us, our intimacy with Zandaye ripened rapidly during succeeding days. She did not neglect her task of teaching us Plutonian; but she had become far more than a tutor; she was a friend as well, and would never hesitate to linger with us overtime and to exchange ideas on all manner of subjects. And so we came to look forward to our hours with her as the only bright spots in a gray monotony.

Yet it was because of her that Stark and I suffered the most serious misunderstandings of all our years of comradeship. It was because of the competition to shine in her eyes that we quarreled, and passed many long foolish hours together in a sulking silence. I shall not tell how dismal and forsaken I felt whenever she smiled upon him; or how moody and depressed he would grow whenever I appeared to be the favored party. It might be too much to say that we were actually in love; on earth, certainly, we would have thought twice before nursing sentimental feelings for a lady who wore a lamp instead of hair, and had two fingers too many on each hand. However, since this was not the earth, she was assuredly the one eligible candidate for our starved affections.

And could it be that Zandaye reciprocated our feelings? If she had not been regarded as freakish by her own people; if her blue eyes had not been laughed at, and her form had not been mocked as grotesque, it is unlikely that she would have been attracted to men of our preposterously lampless build. But no doubt it was a novel experience to her to feel herself admired; and no doubt, being somewhat lonely, she found our conduct less uncouth than our hairy, large-mouthed faces might have led her to expect, and even began to look forward to our meetings. At all events, we noticed that her voice, at our almost daily meetings, had taken on a soft and musical quality it had not possessed at first; while her head-lamp now and then would glow to an ethereal blue, whose meaning we were only able to divine.

But how little we could foresee the strange future of our intimacy. Nothing could have been further from our anticipation than that sweep of events which for a while was to link our fates.

Let me now return to the prosaic question of our food supply, which was becoming more and more of a worry as the days went by. And let me tell how our eagerness to satisfy our palates was productive of many evil fruits, of which Zandaye was to receive more than her share...

One day, turning in disgust from one of our regular meals of synthetic mush, Stark and I left our portions half completed, while gloomily wondering if our weight would not in time sink to the Plutonian standard. We were relieving our feelings by expressing disapproval of the planet in general and lamenting the absence of the art of cooking in particular, when we heard a slight rustling sound, and observed a small grayish creature that had slipped forward to prey upon our unfinished food. Eight-legged, with beady eyes and head-lamp, it was of about the size of a rabbit, and, as we well knew, was one of the numerous varieties of Plutonian domestic animals.

"Suppose it would be good to eat?" I whispered to Stark, seized by a sudden idea. And he, with a wicked gleam in his eyes, muttered, "Wait—we'll find out," and, seizing a steel rod, made an instant end of the creature.

While I had not been prepared for such precipitate action, I freely acknowledge an equal partnership in everything that followed. Clandestinely, like two criminals—as, indeed, we were, according to Plutonian standards—we roasted our prey on the coils of the electric heater that automatically warmed our rooms. There followed a banquet royal, in which we gorged upon the meat, which was tough and stringy but tasted more delicious to us than venison; and after we had licked up the last morsel, we disposed of the remains as neatly as we could in one of the refuse boxes to be found in every corridor, and trusted to good luck to keep the deed undiscovered.

Apparently it was undetected; time went by, and no one mentioned the subject to us. And so, as our fears gradually subsided, we were emboldened to repeat the performance, and then to repeat it once more. Not until we had sacrificed half a dozen household pets did we see any reason to suppose we had acted unwisely.

Then, with the suddenness of a thunder-crash, came the inevitable Nemesis. One day, at an unexpected hour, Zandaye burst in upon us. Her blue eyes, in her excitement, were almost staring out of her head; her fourteen long fingers were working all at once, fluttering in twenty different directions; her head-lamp shone with alternations of scarlet and yellow. At first she was too agitated to speak; she merely sank down into a seat, gasping and exhausted; she panted out a few words that we could not understand, and then for a moment was unable to reply to our bewildered questions.

"Friends—dear friends," she at length managed to say, while her head-lamp glowed to a duller hue and her eyes took on a less terrified expression, "I have come to warn you. I have just overheard a conversation—and one that does not bode well."

"What—what about?" we both demanded.

A brief silence followed; then, with mournful eyes, Zandaye continued:

"Friends, I was passing an open council door of the Committee of Neuters chosen to decide your case. Until today, you may know, there has been doubt as to what was to be done. But now, it seems, an unjust charge has been brought against you—a charge that I for one will never, never believe. By my head-lamp! It is impossible that you, so kind and generous, could have fallen as your accusers say. They claim that you have killed animals—in order to eat them!"

Stark and I attempted no reply. We merely stared guiltily at one another, while Zandaye, not catching the expression in our eyes, hastily proceeded.

"It must be some enemy of yours—some vile enemy who claims that the skin and bones of the victims were found in the refuse boxes in your corridor. How can they believe you would commit such a disgusting deed? Why would you, when you already had food enough? And by my lamp! What an ideal—to eat dead animals! Well, it seems nevertheless that this foolish charge is being considered by the Committee of Neuters. It is even urged as the excuse to perform an experiment which some of them have already been recommending."

"Experiment? What experiment?" we demanded, remembering how murky and dark the lights of the Neuters had become at the close of our recent interview.

Zandaye hesitated, but still wore a frightened expression as she resumed.

"They say that the experiment will benefit you—if you survive. They have been wondering about your lack of head-lamps, without which, they claim, you are not fit for civilized life. Now they argue that you show vicious traits—such as the desire to kill and eat animals—simply because so many things are dark for you and you have no lamps. And so one of our famous surgeons, who is a member of the Committee, is asking the right to perform some operations in order to restore your light. He says he believes that, by removing the lower left half of each of your heads—"

"Lower left half of our heads?" we both interrupted, in one voice.

"So, by my mother's head-lamp, he says! He will then be able to stimulate a certain gland, which regulates the growth of head-lamps, and which he thinks to be atrophied in your cases. By this means, after replacing the removed parts of your skulls—"

"But heavens," I exclaimed, "we will both be dead by then—"

"Not at all," she reassured us, trying to smile. "Not if the operation is a success."

"But how could it succeed?" I raged. "It's impossible…"

"Insane!" snarled Stark.

From her melancholy expression, it was clear that Zandaye agreed.

"But tell me," I demanded, "certainly, certainly this wild scheme hasn't been approved?"

"That's what made me so excited," she confessed, with drooping head and despondent eyes. "It was approved by the Committee of Neuters—just as I slipped away."

CHAPTER TEN
Flight

HAD WE TAKEN days to ponder our course, we could not have reached any other decision than came to us in the next minute.

"See here, Dan!" muttered Stark, lapsing into English in his excitement. "We've got to get out of this hole—and get out fast!"

"Less time wasted the better!" I concurred, in a voice that trembled.

"What's that you are saying, friends?" inquired Zandaye, annoyed that we were speaking in a foreign tongue.

"We were saying," I informed her, in a broken Plutonian, "that we've spent time enough here. We've got to go—get away—escape."

"Escape?" she echoed, while her head-lamp registered a yellow-green flare of dismay. "But how...when...where to?"

"Right now—any way we can. Where I don't know," I sputtered.

"Oh, yes, you do know? You must know," insisted Stark. "There's only one place. We've got to get back to the surface—regain our car—fly away from this accursed world!"

"Oh, if we only could," I sighed.

"But, my friends, you would not leave me?" shrilled Zandaye. "By my seven fingers, you would not go where I could never see you again?"

"We wouldn't want to—not if we could help it," I swore.

"We'd do anything sooner than stay here to be vivisected,"

raged Stark.

"But think, my friends, the Committee of Neuters may yet change its mind..."

"While we still have ours, we won't wait for that," I growled.

"But how do you expect to escape?" inquired Zandaye, whose head-lamp seemed to be ranging through all the colors of the rainbow. "We are deep, deep down in the ground, do you not realize that? Do you not know how far it is, in a straight line, to the highest corridor?"

I asserted that we would cover the distance no matter how far it was.

"Well, it is over thirty cerxes," she stated.

Stark and I performed a rapid mental calculation. "Fifty miles," he computed, with a grim smile. "More than fifty miles underground."

"Nearly ten times the height of Mt. Everest," I groaned.

We had not suspected that we were so far beneath the surface, and the information made us feel as if the weight of the entire planet was bearing down upon our shoulders.

"Well, no matter, it will have to be done," decided Stark, gritting his teeth. "It's our only chance." And then, turning to Zandaye, "Will you—will you be our guide?"

Zandaye hesitated. Her head-lamp flickered, and turned from a faint blue to the yellow of fear.

"My friends," she assured us, in words that wavered and almost broke, "my friends, for you I would do anything at all. But by my father's lamp, it is a horrible risk! There are grave penalties if we should be caught. Perhaps graver penalties for me than for you. But we must not be caught. Yes, I will take the chance—for your sake..."

Once more the blue light returned to Zandaye's head-lamp, while her great eyes shone with mingled benignity and resignation. However, we could not let her sacrifice herself for us.

"No, Zandaye," I dissuaded—and Stark had already opened his mouth for a similar request, "no, you must not take the risk. We will not permit it."

"You must permit it!" All at once the uncertainty had disappeared from her tone; there was the firmness of utter assurance. "You must permit it! How will you be able to find your way without me up through the long mazes? Why, you have not even head-lamps to guide you. How long, do you suppose, before your feet would be entangled in the meshes your pursuers spread for you?"

Stark and I were silent; all too vividly we remembered our recent experiences with the spidery webs in the dark.

"No, friends," she continued, "your only hope is to let me show the way, I have often traveled to the upper galleries; I know all the byways, the side corridors, I will take you where your pursuers would not think of coming. Do you not trust me?"

We were quick to assure her of our confidence.

"Then, by my right of Neuterhood!" was her ultimatum, "you must accept me as your guide! Otherwise, I shall not soon forgive the affront."

As it was far from our desire to affront Zandaye, we let her know that her services were gratefully accepted.

However, there were still many questions to tantalize us. "How can we escape even from our own corridor?" I asked. "I have seen guards watching at the main entrance—and, even if there were no guards, we would certainly be recognized and caught—"

"Have no fear," she counseled. "Sacred head-lamps, do you think I would lead you to the main entrance? I know a small side-passage which is rarely used and where there are no guards, because no one would expect you to find it. Besides—" Zandaye hesitated again, and assumed a meditative expression, "besides, I think you should disguise yourselves. No—by all the powers that see in darkness, you can never be disguised from anyone that looks at you closely. But you may not be noticed at a distance. First, you should cut off all that brown fuzzy weed on your heads and faces."

Stark and I both groaned. Still, when the choice was between our hair and our heads, there was little room for doubt.

"Bring on the scissors," we conceded, begrudgingly. And Zandaye slipped out of the room, and in a few minutes returned with a scimitar-like blade of frightening sharpness.

Now began an ordeal—truly, an ordeal I should not care to repeat. Anyone who has tried to shave with a sword-blade will appreciate how we felt when Zandaye wielded her terrible implement. All in all, when I look back upon that shearing, I feel lucky that we suffered only minor injuries. True, I cursed and grumbled wrathfully when Zandaye, being poorly acquainted with our earthly anatomy, took off the tip of my chin along with my beard; while never have I heard a man howl more belligerently than did poor Stark at the loss of an upper segment of his right ear. Worst of all, Zandaye was horrified at the sight of our blood, which, as she observed, was of a deep red hue; whereas on Pluto only the blood of animals was red, while that of human beings was of the purest blue. I suspect that she had a passing fear that, after all, we were not human.

Nevertheless, she was solicitous in treating our wounds, until finally, after a harassing hour, Stark and I stood completely shorn. Only a bare trace of stubble now remained upon our blood-smeared faces and denuded scalps.

"Now that's better," commented Zandaye, observing her handiwork critically, while she slipped the instrument of destruction back into its scabbard. "Yes, by the lamps of my ancestors, much better! How much more handsome you do look."

Stark and I—observing our shining pates in a hand-mirror passed to us by Zandaye—agreed that we looked like convicted criminals. And so we could only smile grimly when our helper suggested, "You should really go about like that all the time. It's so much more man-like."

"Nothing else we need cut off, is there?" asked Stark, with just a tinge of sarcasm. "Our hands or our noses aren't too long, are they?"

"Well, your mouths are too big," she mused, regarding us with an appraising glance. "Then, also, your fingers are so short, and so few! And your faces are not white enough. But let the eyes of all Neuters be my witness, we can't overcome all your natural handicaps. The most important thing to remember is about your lamps. I really must do something about that. Since you can't have the genuine kind, I must do what I can. Wait just a minute…"

Before we could imagine what she was about to do, Zandaye had slipped from the room again. Not one minute, but many went by before she returned; and meanwhile Stark and I did our best to soothe our still-aching wounds. We knew that Zandaye's intentions were of the best, but we wondered what new ordeal was in store, and accordingly were reassured when she returned with nothing more formidable-looking than two crystal globes.

"Here," she informed us, in tones of ringing satisfaction, "are some artificial head-lamps. They are the kind used by people so unfortunate as to lose their natural lamps by accident. Of course, such crystals give no light of their own, and are worn only for the sake of appearances. However, at a distance they sometimes pass for the real thing."

To our intense disgust, Stark and I now were both equipped with the head-lamps. The process was in no way pleasant; we had first to have some heavy glue smeared over our scalps; and by this means the crystal balls, which weighed three or four pounds each, were fastened so tightly that you might have thought they had grown there. It was long before I could accustom myself to the burden, and it is no wonder that my neck drooped; while Stark, whose neck likewise hung low, looked as freakish as a circus performer with the great gleaming transparent ball staring just above his hairless forehead.

Zandaye, however, was well pleased with the results; in her enthusiasm she leapt up and down for sheer joy, and clapped her long hands uproariously, until we feared that the noise would bring some passing Neuter to investigate.

"Now at last," she exclaimed, "you look like real men. Yes, by the lights of all my family…just like real men! Oh, my friends, you ought to have done this long before. You can't imagine what an improvement it makes in your appearance."

Stark and I grunted, and then consented to having Zandaye put the final touches upon us by rubbing a chalky powder over our lips and faces—as a result of which we looked like walking ghosts.

Now that our makeup was complete, all that remained was to escape. And since Zandaye warned that delay would be dangerous, it was only a few minutes before Stark and I had joined her on the way to one of those obscure, little used galleries that she declared might eventually lead us to safety.

Until the moment of that memorable flight, Stark and I had not suspected the number and intricacy of the galleries that threaded the Plutonian underworld. Hitherto we had traveled mainly in the broad, central corridors, which corresponded to the leading streets of a city; now we were to wander through labyrinthine byways that were like the back-lanes and alleys. To give more than the vaguest idea of the maze of passageways would be impossible, since my memory stands bewildered at the thought. I recall only that we glided through trapdoors and half visible openings in the walls; slunk through dark, grimy spaces reminding me of coal cellars; felt for our way in the winding recesses of tunnels barely wide enough to permit our passage; climbed interminable flights of stairs, and crawled up spiral ascents so steep that we had to go down on all fours. Most of the hollows were of a pitchy blackness; and only the radiance of Zandaye's head-lamp, which shone and glittered like a miniature sun, permitted us to find our way. Before we had been gone half an hour, I began to wonder as to our wisdom in fleeing with Zandaye—suppose that she were to lose her way? Or, worse still, suppose that we lost touch with her? However, even in the absence of such catastrophes, how long would it take us to climb fifty miles to safety?

Yet all my fears, when put into words, only caused Zandaye's lamp to glow to a lavender of amusement.

"By the light of my head...do you imagine I have not thought of all that?" she demanded. "It may cost us a day or two to get out, but we will not starve; I have brought some food with me. Besides, I know a pneumatic tube that will shoot us three quarters of the way upwards in less time than it takes to eat a meal."

Stark and I did not seek the details of the pneumatic tube, although we were told that it operated by means of compressed air. We could not speak much as we continued on our way, each within hand's grasp of the others; we were sufficiently occupied merely in order to avoid the pitfalls of the darkness, and to make sure that no telltale sound betrayed us. Amid the bewilderment of those crazy passageways, it was of course inevitable that minor accidents should befall us; and it is therefore not surprising that Stark should have bruised his knee against some concealed obstacle and ripped his already bursting Plutonian costume till one leg was half exposed. And it is even less surprising that, in bending low to pass through a barely visible doorway, I should have forgotten about my lamp, of which I was reminded by a sudden loud shattering sound, and by a shock through my entire spinal column.

"Cracked! May the Neuters preserve us...your lamp is cracked!" I remember Zandaye exclaiming, mournfully, as she cast her illumination upon me. "Split right down the center—and we can't stop to fix it. Lucky, anyway, it's made of specially tempered crystal; otherwise, it would have burst to bits."

I didn't dare tell her that I wished it *had* burst to bits, since the weight was making my neck and shoulders ache unmercifully.

In silence we continued on our way. Though the air of the galleries was musty, stagnant, and unbearably foul to our nostrils; though the darkness grew increasingly oppressive as the minutes wore into hours, and our fingers became sore from fumbling at the jagged rock walls; though a great weariness overcame our muscles, and our hearts panted warningly as we attempted the difficult ascents, still we felt that we had one great cause for thanksgiving—nowhere had we seen the sign of any foe, nowhere had we heard a suspicious footstep or seen a suspicious light.

"These galleries are seldom used," confided Zandaye, on one of those rare occasions when she let her voice rise above a whisper. "Most of them were built ages ago, before any of the modern thoroughfares. Some have been abandoned, and the others mostly lead to the storage vaults and industrial plants, to which they are a sort of back-entrance. Everyone, however, is required to know all about them, in case of emergency—"

With disconcerting abruptness, Zandaye stopped short. Her head-lamp had lost its sun-white glitter; a faint yellow tinge was overspreading it.

"Yes, what in case of emergency?" I demanded. And then I remembered what a yellow light signified.

"In case of emergency—" she repeated, and once more fell into silence.

The yellow of her head-lamp was growing more pronounced; in a moment, it had turned to a brilliant saffron.

"What is it, Zandaye? What is it?" we gasped.

But still her lamp remained vividly saffron, and she stood stock-still and speechless.

Probably her senses were keener than ours; were able to detect things that we missed. For it was at least a minute—a minute of lingering tenseness and staring-eyed suspense—before we observed, far, far beneath us, a sight that made us shudder. Whole universes away it seemed, lost amid the profound blackness of the long, sloping corridor—but was it not unmistakable, that firefly flutter of a light?

"Come! Quick! We must fly!" Zandaye burst forth, while her head-lamp gave a series of yellow flashes. "Quick! Waste no time!"

You could hardly imagine a madder flight than our ensuing dash through the dark. Zandaye went first, her flickering lamp our guide, her footsteps swifter than ours to traverse the uncertain gloom; while Stark and I panted as best we could behind her, our hearts thumping fiercely as we scrambled up step after sharp-edged step. Still far to our rear, but growing closer, closer, glimmered that firefly light in the dark—and now all at once there was not one light, but three, four, half a dozen!

How strangely, how fantastically rapid their flight appeared as they rose through the vacancies beneath us! At times they would vanish behind some turn in the gallery; then, like torches in a nightmare, would reappear, nearer, more brilliant than before; and always their numbers appeared to be growing!

At last the distance between us seemed to have dwindled to a few hundred yards. The lamp-bearers were advancing by great sweeps and curves, almost as if leaping through the air; they seemed to be making five steps to our one; already we could imagine we saw the baleful glitter of their greenish eyes. Then, just as we were about to sink down in surrender; just as we expected to feel the irresistible seven-fingered hands clutching at our arms, we reached a turn in the corridor, and Zandaye, with cat-like swiftness, flung open a little barely visible door. She darted through; I crept through after her; my eyes caught a vision of fearful lights leaping within hand's grasp; then came the clattering of the door upon its hinges—and darkness!

"Follow me!" my guide whispered into my ear. "They will not find us now!"

However, as I crawled after her through a tunnel just large enough to permit my passage on hands and knees, a staggering thought smote me. Where was the third member of our party? Now for the first time, as my panic began to subside, I noticed that no Stark was at my side—no Stark was to be seen by the wavering light of Zandaye's head-lamp!

"Andy! Andy!" I cried, in terror. But the rumbling cavern echoes were my only reply. "Andy—Andy!" I shrieked again, in growing dread. "Andy...Andy!"

However, there was no response except from Zandaye, who, turning about sharply, put up a warning hand. "Not so loud...not so loud...if they hear you, we too will be caught."

Then, coming close, she whispered a sorrowful confession. "He is gone. We have lost him. I had to do it—he was too far behind! I had to close the door—or we would have been caught. By my lamp! How could I help myself? I had to..."

"So Andy is caught," I groaned. And I fear that the tears

rolled down my cheeks to match those already in Zandaye's eyes.

"But no—it can't be. He can't be caught!" I cried, with insane desperation. "We must go back to him…"

My fury and grief were such that there was no restraining me. Though Zandaye protested that the attempt was madness, I insisted on creeping back through the tunnel on hands and knees; insisted that the door be flung open once more; insisted on scrambling out into the larger passageway.

"Andy!" I cried, hoarsely. "Andy…are you there? Where are you?"

However, the rocky walls flung back that cry as if in mockery. And in all that hollow blackness there was no other answer.

PART FOUR

CHAPTER ELEVEN
Among the Iron Cyclops

IT WAS LONG before Zandaye could persuade me to leave that desolate spot, I moped through the gloom like a man demented; I scarcely cared how I bruised my hands and knees against the rock; I cried out again and again the name of Stark, to be answered only by the sneering echoes and the silence.

"Come away—come away, my friend. They will surely return. They will hear you. They will catch you!" cried Zandaye, whose head-lamp blazed with a terrorized yellow. "You cannot help him now. By the love of all Neuters—you must save yourself! What gain for him if they catch you?"

"What gain for me to escape if he's caught?" I groaned. "What will be the use? I don't want to get away without him. He has been my companion in all my adventures. I would not go back to Earth without him."

"Take courage, my friend, you both will yet escape," predicted Zandaye. However, her words were uttered in the manner of one who speaks of a hope in which she does not believe.

Then once more the heavy silence of those eerie depths fell upon us. It was as though I was paralyzed. I did not know which way to turn, and did not care which way I turned.

Had it not been for Zandaye, I might have gone fumbling back through the darkness; fumbling crazily back in search of Stark, to fall into the hands of my enemies without benefiting my friend. However, Zandaye did manage to dissuade me. Even in this moment of despair, she exerted a strange influence; I felt her presence like a solace, a caressing warmth; and her will, her desire for my safety, was in some inscrutable way a moving force. "Come, we must go!" she seemed to be saying, even when no words came from her lips; and her long, soft fingers, intertwining with mine in the gloom, sent a tremor through my veins, and acted upon me like a command.

And so I had no longer any will, any power of my own. Where she led, I followed—followed unquestioningly, like an infant guided by its mother's hand. With one last disconsolate glance back into the black abysses that had swallowed Stark, I crept with her back into the byway, and for a second time heard her slam the iron door, while the two of us, like conspirators, crawled on all fours through the tunneled depths.

"Where are you leading me, Zandaye?" I felt like asking. "What is to be the end of all this?"

However, I did not put these thoughts into words. My mind was still benumbed; a strange magnetic power still seemed to vibrate from Zandaye, drawing me on as if to some foreordained destiny. And so for many minutes, with her long fingers wound about mine and her blue-white head-lamp serving as our only guide, we groped through that narrow tunnel. That we were bound for some known destination appeared certain, yet, as we stole along our way, with cramped muscles and aching heads, it seemed to me that this dreary pit had no outlet, that we would labor never-endingly through the darkness, that perhaps at last we would be sealed up here like rats.

I can hardly overstate the relief I felt when at length a dim illumination became visible ahead of us.

"There…there! I knew we were getting there!" Zandaye

exclaimed. Then, without another word, she hastened her pace, while every instant the light grew brighter.

"Where are we? Where are we going, Zandaye?"

She did not seem to hear me. Her head-lamp only sparkled more vividly. All at once we rounded a turn in the gallery, my nostrils drew in deep draughts of fresh, life-giving air, and we came face to face with one of the most astonishing scenes I had yet beheld even on this planet of marvels.

Startled, I stopped short like one who, winding through some narrow mountain defile, suddenly comes out upon a panorama of far-flung ranges, forests, valleys, and lakes. My lips opened in an involuntary gasp; my eyes were ready to start from their sockets. Spread out beneath me was a cavern of Titanic proportions; like the one I had already seen, it was at least five hundred feet high and a thousand feet across at its narrowest, while its walls glowed with radiance from some invisible source. However, in all other respects, how unlike anything we had seen before! As far as our eyes could reach, and extending from the floor to the vaulting ceiling, were machines, machines, and more machines. And what machines!

Uncannily noiseless, wheels as tall as ten-story buildings rotated with a slow, deliberate motion. Mile-long chains revolved with only a low, rattling sound; levers longer than the masts of ships bent in and out with a frictionless efficiency; tubes and pipes as thick as the trunks of giant redwoods were twisted and coiled like the entrails of monstrous beasts; wires wound back and forth in a meshwork as of some colossal spider web, and springs as long as a ten-car railroad train were compressed and released with an automatic, mathematical regularity suggestive of incalculable power.

Yet these sights, bewildering as they were, were not the

cavern's most surprising features. Placed at intervals among the wheels, springs and levers, I observed multitudes of what I at first mistook for Plutonian laborers. Each had a head dominated by a glaring light; each showed a slender form from six to eight feet tall, and long thin legs and seven-fingered hands, which flexed and unflexed with amazing rapidity, performing mechanical operations with more precision and dexterity than any man I had ever seen. Only after peering at them closely; only after observing that their movements were too orderly and perfect for mere flesh and blood, did I recognize that they were not living things at all, but cleverly constructed automatons.

"Where—where under the sun can we be?" I muttered to myself, in English, while I still stared hungrily across that incredible scene. And Zandaye bade me repeat the question in Plutonian; after which she attempted to explain:

"I thought you would have guessed. This is the world's chief ventilation factory."

"Ventilation factory?" I demanded. "What do you mean?" The place where they manufacture oxygen?"

"Not at all. That is far away. In this cavern, by means of engines you can't see even the hundredth part of, we start the planet's air in circulation, forcing a breeze down all the chief corridors. Except for this factory, the air everywhere would become stagnant, and after a few days life would be impossible."

"Heavens!" I gasped, whistling in my astonishment.

And then, as the thought of my vanished friend suggested itself to me, I was pierced with fresh grief, and murmured, "I do wish Stark could have seen this. Wouldn't he have been interested? By the way—what are those man-like machines?"

Zandaye glanced at me in surprise; her glittering eyes reproached my ignorance. "Why you silly Lampless thing, they are our workers, of course. The iron men employed in all industries for the last fifty thousand sequons."

"Fifty thousand sequons?" I echoed. And Zandaye smiling tolerantly went on to explain:

"None of the world's factories employ actual human beings any more, except as managers and inspectors. Why should they, when iron men can perform the work so much more swiftly and efficiently? These, you see, never tire; they never complain; they do not object to long hours, they do not go on strike; they do not disobey instructions; they are not known to meddle or blunder. All in all, we estimate that one mechanical man is worth a hundred men of flesh and blood. But the men of flesh and blood have no reason to complain, since they are released for less slave-like work. Now let's be getting along into the factory."

"Just one minute, Zandaye," I begged, glancing apprehensively toward that vibrating wilderness of machinery. "Don't you think we're likely to be seen there—"

There was a laughing decisiveness in her voice as she cut me short.

"Seen? By my head-light…who is there to see us? Surely, the iron men won't notice. No, my friend, this is the one place where we're least likely to be observed, for no one ever comes here except to inspect or repair the machines—which doesn't happen once a sequon, since they are controlled automatically from above. We shall be able to find some recess where we're absolutely safe to talk over our plans. Come, my friend—don't hesitate."

"I'm not hesitating," I denied, with renewed courage; and for a while we spoke no more as we made our way amid the monster machines. We saw the tremendous wheels rotating and whirling above us and to all sides; the huge jointed rods, like the limbs of iron Cyclops, opened and withdrew with a precision beautiful to watch; bellows-like globes, bigger than balloons, were distended and deflated with a swiftness that the eye could hardly follow; screws as large as railroad ties revolved in iron sockets, steel belts twisted and bent about, us, electric coils gave out sparks and flashes like the signals of a wireless system. And all the while, secure from contact with the great machines, we followed a little twisted trail of stone that wound in and out amid the metallic masses like a well-cleared path through a jungle.

Had we clung to that trail, all would have gone smoothly. Unfortunately, it had not occurred to Zandaye to warn me. Can I really be blamed, however, for stepping aside? Can I really be blamed, when the lure was something unparalleled in my experience? Picture a shining crystal ball about ten feet in height; picture its face like a mirror, in which are reflected all the multitudinous activities of the whole vast cavern: the speeding of the wheels, the turns and twisting of the vast chains and belts, the flexing and unflexing of the muscles of all the innumerable iron men. "Can I be dreaming?" I asked. "Do I only imagine all this?" And putting to myself these questions, I stepped forward impulsively to examine the crystal.

So rapidly, so heedlessly did I act that Zandaye's terrified "Look out!" came too late. I did not see the meshes of fine wire on the floor; did not see the long steel rod on the level of my ankles. All that I realized was that my feet, in their headlong dash, struck some unseen obstacle; that I lost my balance, and pitched to the floor; that a sharp snapping sound came to my ears, followed instantly by the most terrific crash I had ever heard...

With detonations as of thunder still resounding in my ears, I picked myself up, stunned, bewildered, but unhurt.

"May the Neuters have mercy on us!" I heard Zandaye wailing. "May they have mercy for what you have done!" But not for several seconds, in my confusion and fright, did I notice the change that had come over the cavern. And when

I did notice, I was scarcely able to believe. Where all had been movement and activity only a minute before, all was now pulse-less and dead. Not one wheel turned, not one belt or chain revolved, not one lever twisted, not one iron man stirred a limb in all that enormous gallery!

Her hands fluttering with fright, Zandaye stood before me open-mouthed. Her eyes were bulging to double their usual size; she was muttering something that I took to be an oath or a curse.

Likewise trembling, I stared at her in speechless confusion. Slowly, mercilessly, in deliberate, incisive accents, like the tones of fate itself, her words were borne to me, "You have done an unthinkable thing! An unthinkable thing, my friend! You have switched off the power...turned off the ventilation supply—the whole world will be without air! By the lamp of the Head Neuter...the whole world will be without air!"

Her words ended in a gasp that was like a moan, and her head-lamp glowed with an alternate yellow and red. And I, gaping at her still half in a daze, was only beginning to realize the enormity of my deed.

CHAPTER TWELVE
A Wrench in the Machinery

LIKE creatures who recognize too late the trap into which they have walked, Zandaye and I gave way to panic as our minds began to grasp the peril of our plight. Suddenly we were filled with the stampeding animal's wild desire to escape; we had no thought but to flee from this gallery, where the great motionless machines everywhere stared down on us as if in mockery.

"Hurry!" whispered Zandaye, the very murmuring of her voice sounded ominously loud. Then, hardly taking time to be sure that I was at her heels, she set off at a sprint down the winding stone walk among the monstrous machines. I had difficulty to keep up with her, for at every turn I risked collision with some outstretched rod or barely visible pipe or wire; indeed, my pace was so impetuous that I could not avoid one mishap, when I came up against a wall with such speed that my head-lamp gave a crash as of a hammer stroke and I saw a crystal fragment clattering to the floor.

Stunned, I picked myself up hurriedly and was about to dash after Zandaye when an unexpected, familiar noise came to me with a flash of fear. It was still faint and remote, but how well I recognized the thick-voiced speech of the lamp-heads!

Zandaye, too, had evidently heard the sound, for she came darting back to me, her head-lamp a glaring yellow. "The Neuters preserve us!" she muttered. "We are too late! They have come already! Quick! A hiding place!"

"But where?" I flung back. And my eyes, searching the desert of wheels and coils, could find no likely place.

Zandaye meanwhile stood staring out across that wasteland, and not a word came to her quivering lips.

At the same time, at intervals, we heard the heavy-toned voices in the distance; gradually they seemed to be growing nearer.

"Here!" exclaimed my companion, with startling suddenness, just as I was about to own myself baffled. "Over here!"

Slipping down on all fours, she cleared a path amid a tangle of wires toward a great boiler-like iron device a few yards away, I followed as best I could; but, being broader-limbed and not nearly so agile, I could pass the wire barricade only after much scratching and tearing, which marked my face and hands with bloody lines and put many a fresh rent in my long-suffering clothes.

Yet I had the best of inducements to haste. The voices had burst forth again, in excited tones; and new voices were to be heard from all sides. And was that not a searching head-lamp that flashed for an instant through a distant gap among the machines?

Reaching the boiler-like contrivance, Zandaye seized a small, barely visible knob and drew open a door leading to a yawning black hollow. Though I was still not within hand's grasp, she slipped through the opening and stood, frantically gesturing. When I came up, bruised and panting, she flung forth seven clutching fingers to hasten my entrance. In a moment, the iron lid had come rattling down behind us.

The interior was not completely dark, for there was Zandaye's head-lamp to illuminate it; and, besides, there were a number of air holes, hardly large enough to see through, though they did admit a small amount of light. Our new quarters, however, were none too commodious; Zandaye and I had barely room to crouch side by side on the iron floor; if I lifted my head it would strike the ceiling, and if either of us moved sideways we would hit the wall.

Yet this haven, such as it was, had not been reached any too soon. Within a few minutes, we heard party after passing party of Plutonians, as they moved in great agitation along the stone aisles all about us. At first, though we strained our ears, we could not be sure what they said, though it was manifest that they were bewildered, alarmed, and angry. We could hear the occasional grating and clattering of tools; could hear explosive exclamations that sounded like oaths or commands, could hear the excitement of the passers-by growing from minute to minute. But we could make out nothing more definite until eventually a group paused to confer only a few yards away.

"By the head-light of my father's father!" someone was saying. "Such a total tie up hasn't been known for a thousand sequons!"

"We still don't seem able to trace its source," a second returned with a groan. "It's just as if some stupid beast had interfered."

"Blessed Neuters, isn't that what did happen once?" demanded a third. "Remember reading of the great tie-up of the Sequon 503,181, in which the world was without ventilation for three days, and two million people perished? Now what did they finally find the cause to be? Nothing but some little household pet, smaller than your hand, which had strayed down here and got entangled in the machinery."

"Yes, by my fourteen fingers, but today the gallery is beast-proof," another voice dolefully added; after which, for a while, there was silence.

"It will be bad for us all at the final investigation," the first speaker sorrowfully resumed. "The Head Neuter will send a committee, and someone will be demoted to the Frigid Corridors. The Head Neuter is very strict about such things."

"But by the glory of his lamp—there's nothing to be done about it now," came the mournful response. "By this time the whole world has noticed the lack of breezes. Why, already, before we came down here, radio complaints about the air supply were coming from a hundred stations. Mothers with babies were frantic, since it's said the lack of a draft kills the very young."

A long-drawn sigh followed by a curse was the only answer; then ensued another silence, and it seemed to us that the party was withdrawing. But suddenly, as Zandaye and I whispered to one another that they were gone, there came an excited whoop, and half a dozen voices began to gibber all at once.

"By my lamp…look at this!" someone exclaimed in astonishment and jubilation. "Just look at this! This little broken piece of crystal! Where did it come from? It couldn't have gotten here naturally."

"Let's see it…let's see!" burst out several eager voices; and all echoed that disconcerting cry. "No. It couldn't have gotten here naturally—couldn't have gotten here naturally!"

With a sinking heart, I recalled the bit of crystal broken from my head-lamp.

"There is no material of this glittering type used in the whole ventilation factory," diagnosed one of the voices soberly, "the texture is different—it must have been brought in by someone—someone who had no license here. Someone who probably caused all the trouble."

"Someone we will have no difficulty in finding, once the Inspection Service gets after him," another added, with an evil chuckle. "By the murky light of his head, I wouldn't like to change places with him."

"No, the Head Neuter is merciless about interference with the air. He considers it the worst offense, next to falsely impersonating a Neuter…now be careful, don't lose that crystal."

There came another ominous-sounding chuckle, and the voices gradually grew more remote.

Meanwhile, huddled against Zandaye in our sweaty iron container, I felt chill after icy chill creeping down my spine.

However, time went by and we were not disturbed. Now and then we still heard some excited party passing, still heard the clattering and thudding of tools, but there was nothing to suggest that our presence had been suspected, or that the damage was soon to be repaired.

And as we waited, Zandaye and I talked in occasional whispers. "What I wonder," she meditated, "is what actually caused all the trouble. The rod your foot pushed against evidently controlled the power, and in your awkwardness you knocked the transmitters out of place and cut off the connections of the electro-radium waves, so leaving the plant without any energy supply. The forces that bless all good Neuters must be with you, otherwise, you would have been burned to death. The damage will be fixed, however, as soon as they find what rod you disarranged—but who can say when that will be? There are thousands of such rods in the factory. If we are not still here tomorrow, and the day after, and the day after—"

However, this was as far as Zandaye could proceed. Suddenly, from without, there came a rushing, whirring sound, accompanied by a chorus of jubilant shouts. And from somewhere above us we heard a clattering as of rotating machinery. Crouched flat against the iron floor, I tried to peer out through one of the air holes; but the opening was so small that I was not quite certain what I saw, and I may only have imagined that I caught a glimpse of great revolving belts and huge levers in motion. "The factory is working again!" I exclaimed, my tones incautiously loud. "It's working! Working!"

Before Zandaye had time to reply, there occurred the most disconcerting event of all. All at once we felt a trembling as of an earthquake; the floor began to shake and shudder, and then slowly was withdrawn from beneath our feet! At the rate of a few inches a second, our only support was sliding away like a folding door into some unseen recess! It was as if some invisible power were pulling the strings, while we, the victims, could only stare and await our doom. With frantic violence, Zandaye reached for the door of our prison, but perhaps her very excitement betrayed her—the handle was stuck! And all the while that she savagely wrenched and tugged, the floor was gliding away, revealing a black abyss. It was only a few seconds before we were huddled together on the remaining foot of our support, which also was withdrawing steadily, mercilessly withdrawing. And the smooth metallic walls offered nothing to clutch at…

In that last horrible instant, we each held instinctively to the other—two drowning persons grasping at the same straw. I felt Zandaye's long fingers weaving themselves about my shoulders; my own arms were flung desperately about her neck. I could hear the violent heaving and straining of her breast as it panted against mine. And thus, clinging together, we fell.

We fell, and in imagination lived through the swift, long drop in the darkness. Yet hardly had our plunge started when we were jarred to a stop. Not five feet below, we struck some hard object with a painful thud, and, still with arms intertwining, lay sprawled upon a sloping surface. All about us the blackness was impenetrable; even Zandaye's head-lamp had been extinguished; it was as if we had fallen into Hades. Yet from the gloom all about us we could hear strange grating and grinding metallic noises; while the sloping surface jerked and jolted like the floor of a railroad car.

In that first startling moment, I was so relieved at alighting somewhere that my terror had almost left me. My head was aching; my sides were sore; one arm felt bruised and strained; a faint trickling as of blood was issuing from my nostrils—but that was all. These facts I scarcely noticed; I was more concerned about my companion, "Zandaye, are you—are you hurt?" I inquired, in a broken voice, as she slowly withdrew from my clasp.

She was a moment in answering, "No—no—I—I don't think so," And then, after a silence, mournfully, "My head-lamp—I think my head-lamp was hurt. I don't seem able to get it to shine."

But the damage turned out not to be serious; after a minute, a reassuring glitter broke through the darkness. By the light of Zandaye's lamp, we could see that we were in a tunnel—a narrow tunnel, little further across than the distance between my outstretched hands. But strangely, its walls were gliding past at prodigious speed!

"By the lower shades...now I see what has happened!" proclaimed Zandaye, slowly, while she hovered close to me as if for protection. "We are on one of the moving freight platforms. One of the platforms used to carry merchandise far down into the depths of the world. You see how steep the grade is?"

"Yes," I sighed. We were descending at an angle of ten or fifteen degrees.

"Evidently our hiding place was one of the containers for factory refuse," Zandaye continued. "As such, it opens automatically at regular intervals, discharging the waste materials on to this platform, which carries them away into the depths."

We were both silent for a moment, staring at the barely visible walls that slipped past us at the speed of an express train.

"How long do you think we will keep going?" I finally

asked.

Zandaye groaned. "Maybe for hours. These freight platforms are not very fast, you see. We will go deep, deep down. Down beneath the Favored Depths, where the cultured and honored citizens live. Down beneath the lowest of the Neuter Circles, straight into the slums! Down, down, down, among the most wretched elements of the population. That is where all freight platforms lead. You will be far, far lower, my friend, than ever in your life before!"

"That comes of trying to get to the surface," I muttered, wondering if I should ever see the open air and the starlight again.

Meanwhile, with terrific jolts and jars, we went rattling on our way. I do not know how much time passed; I had no way of estimating time; I am sure, however, that Zandaye was right in suggesting that we would travel for hours. However, amid all the strain and monotony of that long, dark ride, her presence cheered me in some indefinable way; her voice had a musical ring in my ears, her every gesture had for me a charm that made me feel not altogether unfortunate after all. By insensible degrees, my uninjured arm found its way about her form; my lips moved forward to meet hers, which did not respond, and yet did not withdraw; my words began to quaver with a sentiment they had rarely known before, and I pondered phrases that seemed wild, daring, and wonderfully sweet... And all the while her head-lamp was glowing with the most delicate, the loveliest blue you could imagine.

"Zandaye, what does blue in a head-lamp mean?" I asked, although I had more than half guessed the answer.

Instantly the blue gave place to yellow. Her words came forth by gulps and spasms; she averted her head; had she been an earthly maiden, she might have blushed.

"That—that, my friend, is a question you should not ask," she stammered. "It means—it means I feel—what no one who is to become a Neuter should ever feel. Forgive me—if I feel what I should not feel. I cannot help it—pay no heed. I cannot control my head-lamp…"

"But, Zandaye, is it possible then—is it possible—" I exclaimed, swept by a delirious hope. And my arm was reaching around her, and drawing her closer—when suddenly I was interrupted by a tremendous jolt, which whirled us both forward against the floor. At the same time, the rattling and grating in the tunnel ceased, and the movable platform quivered and grew still.

"At last—the end of the road," whispered Zandaye, as a little unsteadily, we picked ourselves up. "Follow me. We will wait for the proper moment, and then will slip out. By the eyes of all benighted things—you will find we are in a miserable district. But somehow we will escape."

I nodded approvingly; for I saw that Zandaye's lamp had again glowed to a celestial blue.

CHAPTER THIRTEEN
Into the Afflicted Regions

FOR MANY MINUTES we remained in silence on the dark, motionless platform. In the distance an occasional dim light shot up and vanished, but around us all things were lifeless and still. It was not until the platform began to quiver again, as though in readiness for renewed action, that Zandaye seized my hand, and whispered, "Now! Now we can get away without being seen. As you value your head-lamp, waste no, time!"

Without another word, we crept forward on hands and knees through the low-roofed, sloping tunnel. The air, I noticed, was oppressively close and heavy. Foul odors, as of some dank basement, were assailing our nostrils. Fortunately, it was not long before Zandaye's keen eyes made out a tiny doorway in the tunnel wall. "This way," she directed. After throwing open the gate by means of a barely visible little button, she preceded me into a wider and more airy gallery.

A flood of light burst upon us as we entered; we saw that the walls were illuminated by means of large glaring strips of metal strung at regular intervals.

"Ah, now we can safely talk again," Zandaye exclaimed. "We are out of the freight tunnel; no one will catch us here. However, what I still fear is that we may get lost amid the rubbish heaps."

"I don't see any rubbish heaps," I said. Except for the dazzling lights, which were painful to my eyes, the gallery seemed pleasant enough.

"Well, you will see them soon…" she promised. "We are in the slums, the Afflicted Regions—the vilest, most poverty-ridden part of the world. By my lamp…you will hold your nose, all right! But I beg you, do not judge our world by its poorest part. Most of our people are also repelled by these lower realms, and recognize them as a blot on civilization."

Naturally, I was now prepared for something revolting. I didn't know whether I would have to make my way amid actual garbage heaps; yet I had no doubt but that we would encounter men and women of the most squalid and ragged type. However, my fears on another score were quickly quenched. "You need not be afraid of being recognized," Zandaye had insisted, in response to my apprehensive inquiry. "No one down here can see beyond his nose."

In view of my dark surmises, I was astonished to be led into a broad, vaulted corridor magnificent as the palace of a king. More magnificent, probably, than the palace of any earthly potentate! Gold and silver were flung about with a lavishness rivaling anything in *The Arabian Nights*. The walls were patterned of the precious yellow metal, varied by silver and platinum; the ceiling was of gold studded with diamonds, emeralds and rubies; the very floor was of gold interspersed with gems.

"Can it be real?" I gasped, staring like one in a dream. "Can it be real?"

While Zandaye stood gazing at me in perplexity and wonder, I remained as if paralyzed, letting my eyes feast upon that superb spectacle.

"What is the matter with you, my friend?" she at length demanded, a little impatiently, "By the lamps of the sages—one would think you had never seen gold before. Of course it's real. Why shouldn't it be?"

"Good Lord, I—I've never seen anything like it!" was all I was able to blurt out. "Are those—are those diamonds? Are they real, too?"

"Of course...why not?" There was scorn in Zandaye's voice, and her lamp was alternating between an orange of surprise, and a lavender of amusement. "May the light of my head go out, if you don't seem to admire them! You seem to suffer from the same fever as the slum people."

"Slum people?"

"Certainly. Can't you see for yourself that this is the slum district? What else could it be, with so much refuse lying around?"

Swinging her arms about her in a circle, Zandaye pointed to the gold and silver that glittered in every direction.

Weighed down by earthly prepossessions, I required a minute to grasp the situation. Surely, I thought, Zandaye was only joking.

However, it was not in a joking manner that she continued, "This trash here, which is of no real use to anyone, is valued for some queer reason by the natives of the slums. Anybody with a lamp on his head could see that ordinary rock is better for building purposes; while, as for beauty, who would not prefer marble? But the minds of the slum-dwellers seem to be congenitally clouded; it is an inherited disease, scientists say, handed down from those primitive days when the whole world placed value on trinkets. The worst of it is that there seems to be no way of curing it; once a slum-dweller always a slum-dweller, appears to be the rule among these unhappy hoarders of refuse."

While Zandaye was speaking, my eyes were fixed upon a group of passing Plutonians. They were broader of build and bulkier, it seemed to me, than most of the natives; while their head-lamps burnt with singular dullness, and, in fact seemed hardly illuminated at all. However, the most remarkable thing about them was their clothes, which were resplendent with bands and streamers of gold, badges of burnished silver, and precious gems that adorned them by the hundreds and were even visible on the upturned soles of their sandals. The most lavish care was apparent about their whole personal makeup. Their lips were painted in green, moon-shaped curves; their hairless heads were covered with a bluish smudge of powder, and their cheeks were likewise blue-tinged; their ears were weighed down with strings of rubies; and diamonds, sapphires and amethysts dangled in chains about their necks.

"Look, Zandaye!" I whispered, hardly able to contain my surprise. "Who are they...those passing celebrities?"

"Celebrities?" she almost screamed. Her head-lamp flashed to a sudden lavender while she rocked back and forth in babbling laughter. "Celebrities! Great shades of the Lower Depths—my friend has a sense of humor!"

"I do not mean it as humor," I denied, a little resentfully.

"But by my lamp, it is delicious!" flung back Zandaye, still not quite recovered from her merriment. "Why, those people are not celebrities. They are simply poor slum-dwellers!"

As she made this announcement, Zandaye burst again into a babbling explosion.

However, after much difficulty, she did make me realize the Plutonian point of view. The accumulation of gold or silver, she assured me, was regarded by most of her fellow men as a sign of poverty; for a person could at best possess only a certain amount, and if his hoardings were of a material nature, then they excluded those mental and spiritual acquisitions that constituted the true wealth, I could not quite follow the tortuous reasoning that led Zandaye to this conclusion; but I did understand that the disdain of most Plutonians for gold and silver was enormous, and that they flung it to their fellows in the nether regions somewhat as we fling garbage to swine.

So far was I myself, however, from sharing Zandaye's attitude that I regarded the riches on the walls and floors with a covetous eye, and missed many of my companion's remarks in my greed to slip a few valuables into my pocket. It would be a fine thing, I told myself, if upon returning to earth—and in my eagerness I forgot that probably I never should return to earth—I should have a few large emeralds or diamonds to show as the practical fruits of the expedition, I even began to wonder whether, after all, flights to Pluto might not be put on a paying basis; whether our expedition might not prove to be the forerunner of an interplanetary gold rush...

Occupied with such thoughts, I actually had the daring, when Zandaye was not looking, to reach into a corner amid some debris, to snatch a ruby as large as a marble, and to secrete it in the folds of my garment. Assuredly, this would not be my only booty were we to remain in the slums.

After a few minutes, we turned into a larger corridor, whose hundred-foot arching ceiling was a blaze of gold. This seemed to be a central thoroughfare; swarms of the natives were hurrying noisily in all directions—and not one of them but presented of a glorious spectacle, with clothing of gold and silver, or with argent banners and streamers waving after them in the breeze. Even the children, I observed, were adorned with the precious metals, and wore diamonds as earthly children wear glass beads.

"By all the powers of darkness. It is pathetic, how poverty-stricken these people all are," murmured Zandaye. "It makes me want to weep. The worst of it is that none of them seem to realize their plight. Their perceptions have grown dull—notice how poorly their head-lamps shine...

"You see, very little of their illumination comes from within," she continued. "Nearly all of it must issue from outside. That is why there is so much glare and bustle here. But what else could you expect, considering the menial occupations of the people?"

"You don't mean to say," I demanded, "that these

gorgeously robed persons are menials?"

"I mean to say they have menial occupations," she returned, with a melancholy nod. "Isn't it deplorable. What a blemish on our civilization…"

While I was wondering what degrading work the passersby must perform despite their majestic appearance, Zandaye suddenly halted, and pointed through a sumptuous-looking glass partition to a gilded suite of rooms that might have done service for a duke.

"In there—in there they must toil," she muttered contemptuously. "In there they drudge half the hours of their lives. Adding figures…subtracting figures…reckoning profits and losses…speculating, gambling, lying, quarreling, planning favorable trade-balances. Pity them—the poor slaves. By all gracious light givers, isn't it unfortunate that such beings exist?"

Passing a door leading into the splendid suite Zandaye had indicated, I was startled to see a sign…

Bankers, Lenders and Stock Balancers

And across the way, on a door connecting with an equally elegant-looking suite, there was a sign…

Investments, Legal service for hire

I thought Zandaye's wits must surely be wandering.

"The strange thing," she continued, "is that many of these poor benighted creatures choose to remain benighted. No, there is no helping them. We send welfare workers down here to convert them; we promise them all sorts of inducements, even suggesting that some of them, if they show sufficient talent, may be eligible to become Neuters. But it is all of no use. Not one person in a thousand in these lower depths ever rises above his origins. There are, of course, always a few who aspire toward the light, but most are hopelessly submerged in their environment. No career is open to such wretches except to go on accumulating gold."

Not being able to share Zandaye's point of view, I could only grunt a perfunctory reply; while my companion went on to explain, "Some people believe there is an hereditary curse upon these unfortunates. Others think they come of an inferior racial stock, being really cousins to the beasts. Still others hold that they are being punished for sins committed in previous lives. For myself, I cannot say. I only know they are unhappy, and so my heart goes out to them."

By this time we had reached a secluded platinum alcove, apart from the noise and confusion of the main gallery. Zandaye motioned me to sit down with her here, and after we had placed ourselves cross-legged on the floor, she relieved her pockets of a number of capsules and other articles of food, which, however unpalatable, did allay our hunger.

We had just completed our meal and washed it down with the water from a public tap, when we noticed an unusual tumult in the central gallery. With loud cries and gibberings, the people had withdrawn to the sides of the corridor, and were bobbing up and down and waving their hands beneath them in fantastic bows or salaams, while a resplendent large-headed figure walked down the aisle, clad only in the light shed by his own sun-brilliant lamp. Taking advantage of the momentary confusion, I seized a little lump of gold from a cranny in the wall and put it in a safe hiding place; but when I again turned to the spectacle in the gallery, the resplendent one had vanished, although a flock of shimmering-gowned individuals that followed him, in the manner of a military escort, were still trooping by in plain view.

"Who is he?" I inquired of Zandaye, thinking him the most imposing-looking Plutonian I had yet seen. "The Head

Neuter?"

"Head Neuter?" she laughed. "By my lamp what queer ideas you have. Tell me, what do you suppose the Head Neuter would be doing here in the Afflicted Regions?"

Not knowing how to answer, I remained silent.

"No, of course, it was not the Head Neuter," she went on. "But it was someone equally great, or perhaps greater."

"Greater?" I echoed.

"By the radiance of his presence, that is likely. It was probably a poet."

Dumbfounded, I stared quizzically at Zandaye, but not even a ghost, a flicker of amusement illuminated her features. Her face was grave and solemn, and no trace of lavender had crept into her head-lamp.

"It was a poet, doubtless coming here in search of atmosphere," she continued. "You can see how his admirers follow him about."

"But why—why does everyone bow?" I demanded, pointing to the crowd that still bobbed up and down with gestures of homage.

"The Neuters bless you—did I not say he is a poet?" she repeated, as if that were explanation enough.

I must have looked the confusion that I felt, for after a moment she went on...

"Naturally, the poets are the most honored among us. Why should they not be? Do they not lead the world in a far deeper sense than any statesmen? Quite properly, an ancient custom prescribes that they be honored wherever they go."

"But surely down here..." I gasped, too bewildered to control my words, "...down here poets are not—"

"Yes, even here the old tradition rules, as you can see—though it may be that the inner light is so dull that many of the worshippers act only out of habit."

I was just about to make some remark regarding the

impractical standards of Zandaye's people, when a large emerald, which I observed conveniently near at hand, interrupted my train of thought. After a little manipulation, I succeeded in gaining my prize; and at the same time Zandaye, who observed a prize of quite a different nature, startled me by swooping down into the center of the gallery and picking up a small sheet of paper dropped by the last of the poet's passing admirers.

"By my head-light...just look!" she exclaimed, unfolding the paper, which was filled with the jagged-looking native printing. "Just look—a copy of the *Daily Neuter!* All the latest news! I was just wondering what was happening in the world. Down here, you know, they hardly ever read newspapers. They are too busy with the stock reports."

Enthusiastically Zandaye let her eyes race along the contents; while I—having no interest in the news—watched her with a yawn and secretly wished for some good sleeping place. Little did I realize how important that paper was to prove for me.

Suddenly she stopped as if struck. Her mouth opened in a gasp; her head-lamp blazed through all the colors of the spectrum. "By my light, look—just look!" she stammered. "Read—read this!"

However, her eyes darted eagerly down the columns before she would let me have the paper. And, glancing over her shoulders, I read:

RUNAWAY SAVAGE CAPTURED

One of the Wild Men Gets Away in Break for Freedom

The two savages who recently appeared unexpectedly in our midst, and who have given rise to world-wide scientific discussions, have tried to outwit their captors and escape. These aborigines, whose lack of lamps and general low intelligence are only two of their many unremarkable qualities, had been detained recently pending further investigation by a Committee of Neuters, some of whom maintain that, by means of proper surgical incisions, the less human qualities of these visitors could be eliminated and the secret of their origin determined.

After an exciting chase, one of the runaways was captured late today in the Three Hundred and Eleventh Emergency Tunnel by the Inter-Gallery Rangers. The other, according to the Rangers, would also have been taken had it not been for the serious tie-up of the Ventilation Factory, which, by a coincidence, occurred just as the pursuers were closing in on the fugitive. Owing to this interference, the escaped prisoner, who is believed to also be a dangerous lunatic, is still wandering at large; and citizens are urged to be on the outlook for him. He is described as of an extremely ugly and ungainly build; very short and fat; with small weak eyes of a beast-like blue; two fingers missing on each hand, and the other fingers grotesquely short; no head-lamp; an uncouth speech and manner; gigantic mouth of a monstrous red; and a blank but ferocious countenance. Large rewards are offered for his capture, dead or alive.

As for the other member of the pair, he is being held in a strictly guarded cell, and is being subjected to the Ninth Rite of Coercion in order to make him divulge the whereabouts of his fellow, which he is believed to know, but steadily refuses to impart. It is held that, by this method, his resistance will be broken down within a day or two at most..."

"The Ninth Rite of Coercion!" exclaimed Zandaye, her voice shaking, her lamp by turns red and yellow. "May their heads be stricken light-less, but that is terrible!"

Her long fingers clenching and unclenching, and her lamp blazing in angry spurts, she stamped all about me for several nerve-racking moments.

Then, in response to my excited queries, she explained, "The Ninth Rite of Coercion is a survival from our primitive ancestors—an old form of torture, hardly ever used nowadays. The victim is left all alone in a small dark cell, forced to stand upright without food or drink, without anyone to talk to, and without a thing to do. Two or three times a day he is asked whether he is willing to confess—and if he does not answer or answers falsely he is left to his misery for another blank, solitary period. A few days of such treatment is enough to break down a man's spirit if not his mind."

"Heaven preserve us!" I cried. "So that is what is being done to Stark?"

"Yes, by my lamp, that is what is being done…"

I groaned, and a gloomy silence intervened. I pictured Stark in the throes of his lonely torment; pictured him suffering, perishing in his loyal failure to divulge my whereabouts. And as I remembered what a friend he had been, and remembered also our many adventures together, I groaned again, and a sudden resolve flashed over me.

"Come…" I called to Zandaye. "We are going back—at once. I shall give myself up. There is no other way to save my friend."

Zandaye too groaned, and hung her head sorrowfully, but in her great blue eyes there was a gleam of approval.

CHAPTER FOURTEEN
In a New Servitude

ON PLUTO, as on the earth, it is sometimes easier to make a decision than to carry it out. Although I continued to be profoundly agitated about Stark's plight, and knew that only my speedy reappearance could rescue him, I found it no simple matter to make known my whereabouts and identity. Had we been anywhere else on the planet, the problem might not have been difficult; but the people of these golden galleries were flitting back and forth with such haste that I might not have existed at all. They took no notice when I called to them, when I motioned them with excited gestures, or even when I sought to seize them by the arms as they bustled past. And after many minutes of exasperating efforts, during which I felt as if beckoning to ghosts, I abandoned the attempt in despair, and dismally turned to Zandaye for advice.

"By the lamps of all Neuters!" she swore, shaking her head knowingly. "This is only what I expected. I told you the people down here can't see further than their noses. What is more, they are deaf to all sounds except the clinking of metal."

"But isn't there anything at all we can do?"

She nodded, doubtfully. "Everyone here is too much worried over business to care about anyone else's troubles. They have a motto that a helping hand pays no dividends. So, if you value your friend's life, we must look elsewhere. I do not know how far we are from the end of the Afflicted Regions, but maybe if we commence climbing we will soon escape."

There being nothing else to do, I accepted Zandaye's suggestion, and, with a reeling head, started with her through a succession of upward-leading galleries. But for a long while we noticed little change in our environment. Everywhere the walls, floors and ceilings were lined with gold, silver and precious stones; everywhere the natives were rushing past at heedless haste. Some of them, we noticed, carried enormous gleaming burdens around their necks, which hung low as if in shame; others, borne down by no such weights, went gliding round and round in circles, their outstretched hands clutching at emptiness; here and there two or three were writhing and wrestling unnoticed on the floor, tearing at one another with long bloody fingers like the claws of beasts.

Sheer weariness at last put a halt to our search. It was many, many hours since either of us had had more than a snatch of sleep; and finally, we had to pause in a niche between two golden pillars, which, while too hard for comfort, at least did afford us some seclusion. There we both fell into a slumber of sheer exhaustion, from which we awakened I do not know how much later, feeling somewhat sore but otherwise refreshed.

And now Zandaye, who usually made no lamentations on her own behalf, permitted herself a moment of dreary reflection...

"By my lamp! I do not know what will happen to me when we get back. My absence will have been noted...I will probably be reprimanded by my Governing Superior for neglecting my Pre-Neuter studies. If it becomes known that I helped the two prisoners to escape—well, then it is even possible that the Maximum Penalty—"

"But Zandaye—Zandaye," I interrupted, noting the melancholy light in her eyes and the gloomy fading of her head-lamp, "I do not want you to take any more risks for my sake. If it is better for you, we must part at once. Then it will never be known that you aided us. Yes, Zandaye, I fear we must part."

The last words came forth with an effort; I could not but shudder at the thought of separating from my beloved companion.

However, the brilliance came back into her head-lamp and there was fresh energy in her voice as she replied, "By the honor of a Pre-Neuter, do you believe I would desert you? Do you think I would come all this distance with you, only to forsake you now? If so, then do you imagine our people have no sense of right and wrong? Why should I complain of the danger to myself? I faced it willingly; yes, gladly—for did I not face it for *you?*"

"For me?" I gasped; and I noticed how wistful, how tender was the light in those intense blue eyes of hers.

"For me?" I repeated. "For me?" And suddenly I was swept by the consciousness of something strange, something unbelievable. Her head-lamp had again flamed to a heavenly azure; and my intimation as to the meaning of that color was vividly confirmed.

"Zandaye," I murmured; and I allowed my hand to slide into hers, I allowed my fingers to intertwine with her long ones. For the moment I forgot that she was a Plutonian, and I, a native of the earth; I forgot that she wore a head-lamp and no hair, that she had fourteen enormous fingers, and came from a race with manners and ideals alien to our own. All that I knew was that she was a fellow creature, a woman, and one who was infinitely kind and infinitely dear; and at that knowledge, my heart beat fast, my breath came short and hard; and the millions of miles between us were blown away in a flash. And my arms reached forth, and were about to enfold her, would have enfolded her—when all at once she leapt up, freed herself from me, and exclaimed, with resolution in her voice:

"Come! We must not forget ourselves! We have a mission to fulfill! By the mother that gave me birth—how can I listen to you? I know the thoughts that leap in your brain, the floods that stir in your heart. But you must check them, calm them. I cannot listen. For I—I am to become a Neuter!"

With panting breast and head-lamp beatifically blue, she stood facing me proudly, while tenderness tempered by determination spoke in her long, shapely face. As I stared at her, my heart sank even while my admiration and passion grew, for I knew her resolve was irrevocable.

"But, Zandaye," I murmured, in faltering tones, "tell me at least, Zandaye, that I am something to you—that I am—more than the stones beneath your feet..."

"You are more to me than the eyes that give me vision! More than the lamp that shows me the way!" she swore, fervently, although without raising her voice. "Yet you cannot be more to me than my purpose in the world. For that belongs not to me, but to my race... Come now, we must not talk of that any more. Let us waste no time; it still may not be too late to save your friend."

Resignedly I bowed my head. Only too well I realized the truth behind her final words—what right had I to be lingering here, talking of fond and foolish things, when every moment might bring fresh peril and agony to Stark?

And so for many minutes we plodded again along a sloping gallery, and up many a difficult winding and many a long flight of stairs. I noticed that there was a thoughtful glitter in Zandaye's eyes, and that the blue light had not left her head-lamp; and I too was thoughtful, although I did not try to be communicative... But let me pass on to tell how, after hours of walking, we observed a welcome change in our environment, and came out of the labyrinths of precious gems and metals into a still more remarkable district...

Evidently we had been only in the upper levels of the Afflicted Regions; otherwise, we could not have escaped so soon. As it was, however, a series of vigorous climbs took us to a height never reached by dwellers in the Afflicted Regions. No longer was our route lined with gold and silver; no longer did hurrying throngs dart heedlessly past. The atmosphere, as if by some impalpable influence, seemed to grow lighter and easier to breathe; it was as if a weight, a pressure had been removed; and our spirits rose at the sight of galleries that were wider and airier and less brightly but more tastefully illuminated.

I should say, in fact, that never had I seen more exquisite taste displayed anywhere. We roamed through great columned aisles endlessly branching and inter-branching, like those of some colossal cathedral; we gazed upward at gently curving ceilings glowing in a luminous haze; we stared at walls that seemed translucent, crystalline, as though the light, of the hue of moonbeams, seeped through at all points from invisible luminaries. Here and there was a painting, a bas-relief, a statue; and these decorations were neither so numerous as to be ornate, not so few as to be exceptional; but all had the most elegant and imposing simplicity, in which a consummate artistry of design was balanced by an equally consummate artistry of concealment.

"Where are we now?" I asked, while, transfixed with wonder, I roamed through those magnificent halls.

"In the Studio Residential District," Zandaye declared. "H extends for hundreds of miles, and it is all as beautiful as this. This is the region reserved for the most accomplished among the Neuters—the writers of poetry and music and drama, the sculptors and painters, the actors, the architects, the leaders in the dance. It is thought that great art flowers most splendidly among surroundings of great art."

"I don't doubt that," I agreed, thinking that even I might become artistic were I to remain here long. "But where are the dwellers in this superb section?"

Before Zandaye had had time to reply, the answer came from an unexpected source. Out of a small side-gallery, several gleaming figures emerged, evidently attracted by the sound of our voices. They were all exceptional in their slenderness and height, in the size of their heads and the brilliancy of their head-lamps; and all, being Neuters, walked unimpeded by any clothing. Upon seeing us, they burst into a low babbling laughter, pointed to us with curious gestures, and immediately surrounded us; while from half a dozen unobserved entrances their fellows issued, until we found ourselves in the midst of a fair-sized crowd.

About most of these creatures there was something so resplendent, so ethereal that I could almost have imagined myself in the presence of celestial beings. And in their voices, as they turned to one another with excited exclamations that I could not catch, there was a musical softness and resonance not to be found among most of the Plutonians. "Truly, they look like artists," I reflected. Then, remembering the urgency of my mission among them, I attempted to speak—to tell them who I was, and to induce them to deliver me to the proper authorities.

Most of my words, it appeared, were superfluous—these intelligent personages could not fail to know who I was! They were little interested, however, in what I had to say, and my requests bore no more weight than a child's entreaties. After scores of them had examined me with inquiring eyes, and little groups had engaged in eager whispered conversations, one of them—evidently their self-constituted leader—turned to me with long hands uplifted, and announced:

"My friend, you are to dwell among us for a while. It is

true that the Head Neuter is looking for you; but he does not yet know you are here, and will be all the more pleased to find you when you are at last surrendered. Have no fear; we will treat you kindly."

"But I must be given up at once," I cried, despairingly. "My friend must be saved from torment..."

Peculiar smiles flickered across the faces of the artists.

"Do not be alarmed," one of them advised. "We are a humane people; we do not put any man to more torment than he can bear. When your friend reaches the limits of his endurance, the Ninth Rite of Coercion will be relaxed."

There was little enough consolation in this suggestion; yet it appeared useless to argue, I pleaded until my voice was hoarse; then, as a last desperate measure, I reminded my new masters that a reward had been offered for my capture—but they only laughed at the announcement. "What," they demanded, "are we then children, to be moved by the thought of a reward? No—our only reward can be in the advancement of our art. That is why we are holding you here."

How I could advance their art was more than I could imagine; but before long I was enlightened. In the company of fifty or sixty of the artists, amid whom Zandaye walked unnoticed, I was conducted to a large colonnaded court, whose pillars were all of iridescent crystal, and against whose walls a hundred many-colored fountains were playing. A brief intermission occurred, during which Zandaye and I were offered food; and then began an ordeal of an unexpected nature.

The artists crowded about me so closely that most of them had to stand on tiptoe in order to see; while a few, in the rear, elevated themselves upon pedestals or tall improvised platforms. Some, to my surprise, produced palettes and a canvas-like cloth and began to paint; others began modeling out of a dough-like substance; still others made hasty sketches in black and white; while not a few displayed notebooks and commenced to scribble enthusiastically. Yet I was not pleased as I watched the development of their work, and particularly of the paintings and busts, which, I was told, strove to bring out my "underlying spirit," and which depicted me as all mouth and ears, with an expression as humane and enlightened as a gorilla's.

However, not all the artists were trying to produce complete pictures. Some confined themselves to lesser matters. One devoted hours to perfecting an enormous likeness of my nose, not neglecting to bring out the detail of a pimple with photographic reality. Another did nothing but represent my eyelashes. Still another portrayed my teeth, which—being much larger and more numerous than the native variety—were regarded as curiosities. But most remarkable of all was one who made pictures little larger than a postage stamp, to which, upon their completion, he applied a little buzzing electrical tube.

"This magnifies the illustrations a hundred diameters, and makes it possible to flash them all over the world," he explained. "Whenever I give the release signal, people in every far-off gallery will instantly see your eyes, your ears, your lips represented upon a screen…"

If this was fame, surely I should have enjoyed it. Yet never was I more bored than in those long hours when I served as an unwilling model. The worst of the matter was that one sitting did not suffice; I was forced to pose several times; I was detained for days, and was so well guarded that there was no possibility of escape. And meanwhile what unbearable pests were harrying me! I think the most irritating were the novelists, who insisted on examining every hair of my body in order that they might omit no detail from their realistic stories; but the musical composers were nearly as bad, for they desired to represent my prevailing mood in symphonies which, while generally applauded, sounded to my inexperienced ears like the rattling of kitchen dishes. The poets, again, made my life a misery by their greed to celebrate in verse the "shades and nuances" of my thought; yet, from all that I could gather, they had more to say about the shape of my arms and feet than about anything that went on within. As examples, let me quote, as nearly as I can translate them, some stray lines that come back to memory out of the many composed in my honor:

O creature of the blue-eyed, Lampless head,
Who breathes, yet walks in darkness like the dead. You come
among us like a ghost to show
How our wild forebears, age on age ago,
With idiot faces, gaping and inane,
Were monsters, gross of build and weak of brain.

I freely confess that such lines did not fill me with any enthusiasm for Plutonian poetry. However, I dared not be critical, since I realized that I knew nothing of the higher arts; I merely grumbled a bit and kept my own counsel, while whole reams of similar effusions were being prepared for world-wide distribution.

It will be believed, therefore, that my eagerness to reach Stark was not my only reason for rejoicing when at last I was informed that my incarceration among the artists was approaching its end; that the Ruling Neuters had been notified of my presence, and that, along with Zandaye, I should be sent for on the following day.

PART
FIVE

CHAPTER FIFTEEN
The Ninth Rite of Coercion

AFTER BIDDING our artistic friends a none-too-regretful farewell, Zandaye and I were placed upon another movable platform, and went whirling away for scores of miles through a darkness illuminated only by Zandaye's head-lamp.

"I do hope we're not sent before the Head Neuter. By my lamp—I do hope we're not!" she kept repeating, as we clattered along our course. "How would I ever live down the disgrace?" And I, trying my best to console her, allowed my arm more than once to slip around her waist; though always she would gently disengage herself, and remonstrate, "No, no, my friend, you must not. Were I not to become a Neuter—then it would be different. But now, of all times; now, when I am under suspicion, and perhaps will soon be under trial, I must behave worthily. Embraces are not permitted to Pre-Neuters."

Even as she spoke, her head-lamp glowed to a beautiful blue that belied her words and gave me reason to believe that, with a favorable turn of fortune, my pursuit would not be hopeless.

Suddenly, though, I recalled my own predicament; recalled that I was being summoned before I knew not what judges to answer for my flight—and that I might undergo a brain operation from which there could be no recovery. At the same time, I thought of Stark, who, for all I knew, might have succumbed already to his tormentors; and remembering him and wondering in what condition if at all I should see him again, I was filled with an overwhelming impatience to reach the end of my journey, to see my old friend, to know that all did not go so badly with him as I had imagined... And so the minutes seemed hours, the hours age-long before the termination of our rattling ride in the dark.

But at last we did jerk to a stop. A door was flung open, and a torrent of light was flashed upon us; we heard a tumult of voices, and saw a wavering of head-lamps; then several long-armed individuals stepped forward, and, ranging themselves as captors about us, led Zandaye and me down miles of dark, sloping corridors.

I half believed we were now on our way to the Head Neuter; and so did Zandaye, to judge from the yellow glow of her head-lamp. The sequel, accordingly, was to be a welcome surprise. Passing a doorway guarded by one of the monstrous domestic animals, with the six long legs, the huge greenish mouth and the crocodile-like teeth, Zandaye and I both cried out in sudden joy. With a delighted cry, a well-known figure rushed forward to greet us!

It was Stark—Stark, alive and well! The first glimpse showed us that he was unusually thin and pale; but at least he had survived. "Dan...Dan...and Zandaye, too!" he exclaimed in a faltering voice, apparently sharing in our surprise—and his hand shot out and seized mine in a clasp such as I had rarely felt before.

"But, Dan," he bubbled over, as soon as he was able to speak halfway coherently. "Dan—I—I didn't expect to see you, I—I thought you were being sentenced to the Ninth Rite—"

"Ninth Rite of Coercion?" I finished for him. "What! You mean to say—"

"Mean to say you weren't sentenced to it at all?" he interrupted, in a flustered way. "Why, they told me—"

"They told me you were going through it yourself," I

broke in.

"Then they told us both the same story!" he shrilled, and joined me in sudden laughter.

By this time our captors were passing from the room, leading the mournful-eyed Zandaye away with them. Stark had barely had time to press her hand, and I had barely had a chance to motion her a hasty farewell before she had glided out of sight.

Sobered by her disappearance, I listened in a solemn mood as Stark went on, "Why, I *am* stunned. Here they have been telling me that you were captured and being submitted to the Ninth Rite, which wouldn't be relaxed until I'd told where we'd come from. Picture my predicament, Dan—at first I actually kept repeating the truth—that we came from a far-off planet—which aroused the lamp-heads first to amusement, and then to anger. It was impossible to make them take my statements seriously; they insisted that we must have come up from the unexplored bowels of their own world; and I was racking my brains to think of some plausible lie to save you."

"At the same time," I cried, "I was giving myself up to save you…" And I mentioned the printed report that he was being tortured.

At this Stark looked puzzled for a moment; but soon an explanation flashed over him. "Can't you see, that was just a ruse?" he pointed out. "By Jove, they thought you might read the newspaper article, and if so, you'd be fooled, and give yourself up."

I nodded dismally in reply.

"Now Andy, tell me what's been happening to you all this time?" I demanded, after a moment. "Let's hear the whole story."

"Why, there isn't so darned much of a story," he declared, reflectively. "You know as well as I do what happened in that tunnel when we were trying to escape with Zandaye. In our crazy rush, I stumbled over some invisible object, and the few lost seconds made me lag far behind, I don't know whether you saw me fall, for you and Zandaye dashed on and on—"

"No, this is the first I knew of it."

"Well, at any rate, I thought I saw you creeping through a small hole in the tunnel wall ahead of me. But before I had come up you were out of sight and those wolves of pursuers were all around me. In that terrible second, luckily, I didn't lose my head; when they seized me and demanded where you had gone, it came to me to point straight ahead and put them on the wrong track. Their top-lamps were flaring in a way to show intense excitement; and evidently they were too much agitated to notice the false note in my voice, for they did dart with me straight ahead through the long gallery. Of course, they didn't find you, and their lamps became red-hot with rage, and they made all sorts of threats when they began to suspect that I'd duped them. But I pleaded that I couldn't know what side-path you had taken, and they started back with oaths and growls, and, I believe, would still have found you—if they hadn't heard some exciting news at about this time. The whole planet's ventilation system was out of order! Then you should have seen the stir and commotion! My captors seemed to lose their heads completely; they acted like men aboard a sinking ship; they shrieked and yelled that they were all going to be suffocated, and for a while seemed to forget me altogether. This offered an opportunity, and I was planning to escape again, and was already slipping away— when, as bad luck would have it, the ventilation started again, and I was caught sneaking off into a little side-gallery."

In a cautious whisper, I mentioned my part in interfering with the ventilation; and this pleased Stark so much that he enjoyed another long spasm of laughter.

"Well now, having been captured," I went on to ask,

"what you been doing all these days? Evidently you haven't had a bad time of it?"

"No, not very bad," he admitted, pointing with a shrug about the spacious, well illuminated room. "I've been right here pretty nearly all the time—and can't complain about my treatment. The lamp-heads have lent me all the books I wanted, and would come in now and then to talk; but of course there wasn't any hope of escape. You saw that six-legged black brute at the entrance?"

I nodded.

"Well, he's a sort of watch-dog. At any rate, he's posted there at the door all the time—and never takes it into his great stupid head to desert his post. Once, when I tried to pass him, he made such a dash at me with those crocodile teeth that I broke all speed records getting back into the room."

After I had heard Stark's story, he wished to learn of my adventures; and so I consumed the better part of an hour in telling of my experiences in the Ventilation Factory, the Afflicted Regions, and the artistic district. To all this he listened with intense interest, but from time to time a wistful smile crossed his face, and it was clear that he envied me my long companionship with Zandaye, as well as my acquaintance with strange and far-off parts of the planet. He was particularly impressed when I described the lower levels, with their golden corridors; I can still picture how his large blue eyes almost popped out of his head at sight of the precious stones and the lumps of gold which I had secreted in my garments and now displayed with furtive gestures.

"When we get back to earth," he declared, as he carefully examined the gems, turning them over and over as if to make sure they were genuine, "we will have these as evidences of our accomplishments. Aside from their value, they will be souvenirs—

However, he suddenly broke short. "However, *will* we ever get back?" he lamented, shaking his head sorrowfully. "Will we ever, ever get back?"

"Yes—will we ever get back?" I echoed. And for a moment we were both silent, absorbed in melancholy thoughts.

"I don't know why they're holding us here," Stark at length resumed, meditatively. "But certainly it is not on account of our beauty. We can thank our stars if we don't face the very fate we tried to run away from."

Yes, and what's more, our record in running away won't help us," I mourned. "If only Zandaye too doesn't suffer."

Before Stark had had time to reply, we heard a commotion of voices from without, and the door was flung abruptly open.

"This way, please!" bellowed a shimmering-robed individual, thrusting his head through the door. "The Committee of Neuters desires to see you—!"

CHAPTER SIXTEEN
Condemned

WAN-EYED and trembling, Stark and I arose, and exchanging dismal glances, hastened out into the corridor, where half a dozen attendants were waiting.

In their company, we made a journey of many miles, partly on foot but mostly on traveling platforms, and at length were conducted into an enormous, high-ceilinged hall, in whose gleaming recesses hundreds of Plutonians were squatted or sprawled upon the floor. Upon our arrival, they all sat up as if at attention, and uttered low cries of pleasure; while we, taking no heed, passed on down the aisle to a wide elevated platform at one end, where we were bidden to be seated. We noted with surprise that the platform had only one solitary occupant—none other than Zandaye, whose head-lamp glared with a yellow of dread, and whose eyes were moist as if with weeping. We nodded to her, and she made mournful acknowledgement, but since our captors took seats within hand's grasp, there was little that any of us could say.

Fortunately, we had only a few minutes to wait. Then a sudden commotion became manifest; as if at some common signal, all the waiting hundreds of lamp-heads leapt to their feet. They flung their long arms enthusiastically toward the ceiling, waved, and gesticulated; their voices were lifted in an excited shouting, then became blended in the tones of a tumultuous song, of which all that I could catch was a line beginning:

"The Neuters come, they come!"

As these words dinned in my ears, I noticed a group of ten unclad dignitaries gliding into the hall with brilliantly sparkling head-lamps. Slowly and sedately they approached, while the chanting and the wild gesticulations continued; straight toward us they walked, and, mounting the platform, ranged themselves on the floor only a few yards from our attendants and ourselves.

Now by degrees the uproar subsided, until at last the whole hall had fallen into silence—a silence that, contrasting with the pandemonium of the moment before, bore down upon us like something heavy, threatening, portentous. Nor was the evil spell relieved when the hush was broken by the most august-looking of the new arrivals. Designating Stark and myself with a seven-fingered hand, he demanded, in husky tones of terrible volume, "Let the business of the day begin! Bring the prisoners before us; let us hear the charges, that we may pass sentence, releasing the innocent and condemning the guilty…"

So still, so silent had the audience become that, for a moment, had I closed my eyes, I could have believed myself alone in empty space.

Then, ending the tenseness of the interval, there came the voice of one of our attendants, who spoke with head abased as if in prayer:

"O Lord Neuters, never for many sequons have we had any more important cases to be decided than today. Never, indeed, since that historic trial, which no man now living is old enough to recall, when a newly made Neuter broke the vows of his Order and sought, by surreptitious means, to find a chemical formula to restore him to male hood and the woman he loved. Following the judgment in that classical case, when the penalty was such that no one has ever dared repeat the offense, it has not been given to any Committee to decide any matter so vital for the welfare of the ruling sex as that which is placed before you today. Shall I proceed, O eminent Lords?"

"Proceed…" ordered the august-looking one.

The heads of all the audience were craning forward eagerly; hundreds of lamps scintillated with white sparks and flashes. But Zandaye's luminary was of a fluttering yellow, and my own—had I possessed one—would probably have been more brightly yellow still.

"We have today three persons to be tried," continued the attendant, in oratorical tones, while poor Zandaye averted her eyes and hid her face for shame. "Two of them are not natives of our land, and I will not presume to say of what land they are natives, although they are sometimes known as the Half-Men, and sometimes as the Missing Links. The other is one of our own citizens, and one who has already risen to the honorable position of Pre-Neuter. Her name, in fact…" here the speaker paused long enough to glance at a bit of paper in his hand, "…is Zandaye Zandippar, Pre-Neuter No. PX 285 AZ. She is charged with being a collaborator in the crimes of the two other defendants. Shall we consider her case first?"

"By all means," snapped the judge. "As one of our own citizens, she has the right to be sentenced first. Now, Pre-Neuter PX 285 AZ, will you take your place before us?"

Slowly and falteringly, with head-lamp still a pitiable yellow, Zandaye arose and faced the ten dignitaries.

"What are the specific charges?" bawled the leading Neuter.

Another silence followed, while the head-lights of the audience sparkled more brilliantly than ever. Then slowly and portentously the attendant opened a long roll of paper, and began to read:

"Zandaye Zandippar, Pre-Neuter PX 285 AZ, of the class of the Sequon 996,433 D. F., is accused of facilitating and abetting the revolt of two prisoners known as the Lampless Ones, alias the Ten-Fingered Barbarians, alias the Big Mouths. She is charged with having neglected her Pre-Neuter studies for a period of not less than eight or ten days, absenting herself even from the Bi-Sequonal examination on Neuter Ideals and Accomplishments. She is also alleged to have penetrated into the Afflicted Regions, where no Pre-Neuter is allowed without a special visitor's blank; while it is claimed that subsequently she loitered without a permit in the Studio Section, where she was found in the company of the Lampless Ones, alias the Weedy-Headed. Aside from that…"

"That will do!" interrupted the judge, severely. "The charges I have already heard are sufficient, if proved, to justify the maximum penalty. Well, PX 285, what have you to say?"

Poor Zandaye, it appeared, had very little to say. Her head-lamp flickered and almost went out, then burst into an irregular series of yellow sparks; while her voice, faltering and unsteady, could barely utter, "I—I—my Lord Neuter—I know the charges are all true. But—but there are extenuating circumstances."

"What's that?" bellowed the Lord Neuter. "Extenuating circumstances for violating your Pre-Neuterhood?"

The audience leaned forward more breathlessly, more tensely than ever; while in the greenish eyes of the ten Neuters there was a hard, accusing light.

"I—I—I wanted to help the other two prisoners," stammered Zandaye. "They—they were strangers in our land—and I wanted to help them. I—I did not think it would harm anyone—and they were so helpless, and so much in need of me…"

"Is that all?" thundered the spokesman of the Neuters. "Was there no other reason?"

"No, no other reason," denied Zandaye.

But as she spoke, unfortunately, a tinge of blue came into her head-lamp, to vanish almost instantly. It was only a flash, and many an eye would not have observed it at all; yet none of the Neuters seemed to miss it or its possible meaning.

"PX 285, you need say no more—" howled the magistrate, while his fellow Neuters cast shocked glances at one another. "You have betrayed yourself! You have revealed a tender sentiment forbidden to all Pre-Neuterites. Hence there can be but one possible decision. What do you say, colleagues?"

All the assembled Neuters solemnly nodded, and their leader went on to decide, "I grieve to pass judgment, for it troubles me, my child, worse than it does you—particularly in view of your extreme youth, since you cannot be more than sixty or seventy sequons old. But the law is the law, and must be respected; though only twice before, in all my five hundred sequons of service, have I been obliged to perform a similar duty. Therefore listen carefully, PX 285…I prescribe the Maximum Penalty. You must give back your pledge of Pre-Neuterhood, and pass the rest of your days as a female!"

Even the hard greenish eyes of the judges seemed moved to pity at the blood-curdling scream that followed these words. Even the spectators were softened to tears as Zandaye uttered that terrible cry, and then, her whole form suddenly limp and lifeless, fell helplessly to the floor.

But after a few minutes, during which the spectators crowded forward and there was much excited fluttering back and forth on the platform and restoratives were hastily applied by the Neuters, the stricken girl managed to open her eyes again, although in a wan, weak way, as though the sight of the world had suddenly become unbearable to her.

"She will be all right again in a little while," pronounced

the chief of the Neuters, unconcernedly. "Let her be borne out and allowed to rest. Now we may resume the hearing."

Gradually the spectators settled back to their seats on the floor; gradually the Neuters glided again into their places; gradually order was restored while Zandaye, supported by two attendants, was led tottering from the room.

However, neither Stark nor I, as the moment of our own ordeal approached, cared very much about the results. For it was because of us that Zandaye had been condemned; and our own fate seemed a minor matter while we still saw the torment in her flooded blue eyes and heard her disconsolate cries ringing in our ears.

CHAPTER SEVENTEEN
Surgical Justice

FROM THE portentous silence that followed Zandaye's departure, and the vivid manner in which the head-lamps of the spectators glittered, we could see that the curtain was only beginning to unroll on a long-awaited scene.

It was with an impressive slowness of manner and an impressive drawl that one of the attendants arose, opened a long scribbled document, and commenced to read:

"Now we come to the case of the Lampless Ones, alias the Brute-faced, alias—"

"Here, let us waste no more time," thundered one of the Neuters, interrupting with a scowl. "The prisoners, I am told, have no less than sixty-one aliases! Let them be designated by name or number."

From the audience there came a low approving murmur.

"Illustrious Lords," answered the attendant, apologetically, "among the many things which the prisoners lack are names. It is true that they have asked to be called by some barbaric combination of sounds, which offend the ear and which of course we cannot heed. Their numbers, however, have been recorded. If you will wait, I shall find them."

A long, tense minute passed, while the attendant searched the papers in his hand.

"By my lamp, here we have it," he exclaimed at last. "Unclassified GH 1987 XZ, and Unclassified GH 1987 A-XZ."

"Very good," nodded several Neuters in chorus. "Now proceed..."

The attendant accordingly read:

"The prisoners are accused on thirteen counts, of which the first is that they have come to the Neuter Corridors without legal permission, and have refused to explain their origin, other than to tell some story regarding different worlds, which would fail to deceive the intelligence of a child. The second count is that, for some strange reason, they have killed several of the small domestic animals known as Rahtios, scorched the flesh, and used it as food—"

Murmurs of horror escaped from the audience in such a chorus that the reader had to pause.

"What is that?" burst forth the husky voice of a Neuter. "H it necessary to read all these revolting details? Can you not spare the sensibilities of your hearers, and pass over all examples of moral flagrancy and crimes against nature?"

The reader bowed his head, and acknowledged, "It was written here on the paper, O distinguished Lords, but I should not have defiled my lips by mentioning such abominations. If you will not graciously accord me your pardon, I will willingly suffer the just penalty under the Anti-Ugliness Statute."

"Proceed..." pronounced one of the Neuters, magnanimously. "You are pardoned."

Meanwhile Stark and I, inwardly writhing, sat staring at one another with hopeless glances. If the lightest of our offenses had been received so sternly, what would be said of our more serious breaches?

"Count three..." The voice of the reader rang out with accusing severity while the hundreds of spectators leaned forward with the relish of onlookers at a play. "Count three. The prisoners, though well and courteously received, though housed and fed like our own citizens, and though about to be accorded medical attention which would have removed their natural deficiencies, are charged with having violated our hospitality and entering the Inter-Gallery Depths by means of the Forbidden Tunnels, where one of them was arrested by the Inter-Gallery Rangers; while the other—Unclassified GH 1987 A-XZ—had not the good grace to yield to his pursuers, but escaped to commit even more gross violations. Shall I read the specific charges, O majestic Lords?"

"Read them!" bawled one of the Neuters. "That is, if they be not unmentionable."

"They are nearly so," testified the attendant. "Yet I may have to continue, though my tongue recoils before the very monstrosities I must utter. Count Four. Unclassified GH 1987 A-XZ, having broken into the Ventilation Factory, where not even a Neuter is admitted except in cases of worldwide emergency or under a special permit from the Governing Council, repaid the good that had been done him by evil, and, by cleverly disarranging the ventilation machinery, cut off the world's supply of fresh breezes and precipitated a crisis that might have cost millions of lives had the ventilation not soon been restored."

The speaker halted, and an ominous silence fell. It seemed to me suddenly as if I were the target of a thousand eyes, all ablaze with a green anger and malice.

"Count Four," proclaimed the spokesman of the Neuters, in slow, significant accents, "is by far the most serious of all. It is clear how depraved any individual must be before he would attack the young and helpless, and deprive millions of invalids and infants of their fresh draughts. I will not believe such a charge without evidence. Unclassified GH 1987 A-XZ, is it true that you deliberately planned to tie up the Ventilation Factory?"

Such was my bewilderment that it was a minute before I

could reply; and meanwhile the silence and the stares of the Neuters and the spectators bore down upon me like some mad terror in a nightmare. In my dismay, I could not believe that my presence in the Ventilation Factory had actually been discovered, could not think that my accusers were making more than a shrewd guess. At the same time, I was enraged to feel how my intentions had been misconstrued.

"No, Honored Lords, it is not true that I planned to tie up the Ventilation Factory!" I surprised myself by exclaiming, as I shot to my feet. "Nothing could have been further from my desires! What would I, a stranger in your land, know of your Ventilation Plant? There is no evidence! I assure you, Honored Lords, there can be no evidence..."

"No evidence?" The cry was flung back at me like a challenge. "You say there is no evidence? By my lamp—let us see! Noble Lords, let us see..."

Springing to his feet, one of the attendants approached me with arms brandished as if in a threat, while a little crystal object glistened between two of his outstretched fingers.

"Look...look here," he scolded. "Let us make the test, and discover whether there is no evidence!"

At first I had no conception what he meant; but during his ensuing speech an illumination burst upon me.

"Look—look, august Lords," he continued, while the eyes of the Neuters glistened with excitement, and agitated murmurs sounded from all points of the hall. "Here is a piece of crystal picked up in the Ventilation Factory just after the recent tie up. Upon its discovery, it was evident it had been left by the intruder responsible for all the trouble; for no crystal of this glittering type is used in the Factory. Moreover, it was found, upon microscopic examination, that it was the sort of material in use for artificial head-lamps, and for no other purpose. And since artificial head-lamps are very rare (not one person in a million being so injured as to need them), it was easy for the Tabulation Department of the Government to trace all the wearers of such accessories in this part of the world. The search, I need hardly say, was swiftly conducted but we found no person from whose head-lamp this fragment might have been broken. Naturally, we were baffled, until, upon capturing the second of our two prisoners, GH 1987 A-XZ, we discovered that he not only had an artificial head-lamp, but one that had had a piece chipped off in an accident. All that now remains to be determined is whether the particle in our possession matches the fracture in his head-lamp."

"Good—good!" exclaimed several of the Neuters, in chorus. "Very good—excellent!" And their long hands fondled their chins in evident relish; while from the audience came mutterings of anticipation and delight.

As for me, I prayed for nothing more fervently than to be safely back on earth again. All too vividly I recalled the accident in the Ventilation Factory, which had deprived me of a portion of my head-lamp.

"Now for the test!" announced the attendant with the bit of crystal as he approached to within hand's grasp. "Now for the final evidence…"

Then, while I shivered and shrank from before him, and felt the hundreds of pairs of glittering eyes aimed at me like daggers, his hands reached down and I heard a clicking sound as the piece of crystal was adjusted to my head-lamp.

"Did I not tell you?" he exclaimed, triumphantly. And all the Neuters, forgetting their dignity, crowded forward to examine. "As you value your lamps, observe for yourselves…it fits like a key into a lock!"

"Like a key into a lock!" echoed several voices. "Like a man into his own skin."

While the Neuters were returning to their seats and the ex-citement of the audience was gradually subsiding, it seemed to me that my last moment was at hand.

It was in a grave, slow voice that the leading Neuter at length broke into speech; but I was relieved to observe that his head-lamp did not show a red flame, although there was something a little menacing in its alternate tinges of green and purple.

"Prisoner Unclassified GH 1987 A-XZ, has been proved guilty of an offense as rare as it is grave. It is an offense that, in the case of one of our own citizens, would justify a penalty of two hundred and fifty sequons of menial labor in the Frigid Corridors. As a just court, however, we cannot sentence him as we would one of our own citizens. We must take into account mitigating circumstances, such as his lack of education and opportunities, the inferior brain with which nature has endowed him, and his natural inability to distinguish between right and wrong. Above all, we must consider his lack of a head-lamp, without which he is unable to find his way in dark places. It is conceivable that his crime was committed not because of the viciousness of his nature, but because of an inborn mental and spiritual blindness. Now as everyone knows, the first maxim of jurisprudence is that we should never try to punish that which can be cured by medicine; hence the present case should perhaps be left to the physicians. So, at least, one of our colleagues contends, and I think we should hear his voice."

The speaker ended, and with a courteous gesture designated a particularly tall and slender Neuter seated just to his right.

"That is true," confirmed this individual, in a voice that re-minded me of a radio with too much volume, and while an icy wave seemed to sweep across the room and envelop me, he continued:

"As a Neuter who has devoted six hundred sequons to the study of surgery, I have naturally developed my own theories;

and the chief of these, with which most of my confreres will agree, is that all maladies, whether of the body or the mind, can be cut out by means of the knife. Now let us consider the two prisoners. They both display an unhealthy, not to say a badly diseased spiritual state, since both of them have shown a habit of killing and eating animals; while both have tried to escape our hospitality, and one has been guilty of impeding ventilation... But how can we remedy all this? Suppose that we condemn them to the Intolerable Corridors for a few hundred sequons—is it likely that they will be reformed? No, to the contrary; their brains will remain at their present low level; they will not have risen above their present evil ways of thought.

"Let us therefore go to the roots of the matter, and try to remake the brains themselves. I will admit that at first sight the case will seem hopeless, but, as the records of medical science prove, imbecility is not immune to treatment. If we are able to stimulate the Superlampular Gland, which controls the head-lamps, we may yet be able to make their organs grow in a normal manner, so giving them the correct vision that they so desperately need. The operation, I am very happy to say, is a comparatively simple one. We need remove no more than about ten square inches from the lower left-hand corner of the skull, following which we will cut our way through perhaps two, maybe as many as three inches of the cerebral matter—"

This was as much of the speech as I was able to hear. Stark had given a low gasp and fallen half-lifeless at my side; and I occupied the next two or three minutes in the effort to revive him.

However, I too was nearly in a swooning state by the time I could turn my attention again to proceedings in the hall.

The first thing I now observed was that the Neuters were all nodding approval of the recommendations of the surgeon, who had just taken his seat.

"Well, prisoners, before we pass judgment, have you anything to say?" demanded the High Chief Prosecutor. "If you know of anything that is more for your good than the sentence we are about to impose, now is your time to speak!"

Despite the faintness that had overwhelmed me the minute before, I managed to struggle to my feet.

"O renowned Lords," I found myself able to plead, "I do not doubt that your eminent surgeons are skilled in their profession, but in the land where I come from it is not considered wise—no, it is not even considered safe—to make incisions in the brain—"

"Not wise? Not safe?" interrupted the physician. He laughed a sly, mocking laugh while his head-lamp glowed faintly red. "A lamentable superstition, dear friends. A relic of the Black Ages. But perhaps the prisoners themselves are still in the Black Ages. Why, we offer both of them, free of charge, an operation that most citizens would have to pay for with half a sequon's labor. And yet they object! What base ingratitude, my Lords."

At this he laughed another sly, derisive laugh; and then, slapping his knees with his tendril-like fingers, fell into silence.

But fighting down my indignation, I proceeded with my appeal:

"If you say that you are acting for our own good, O worthy Lords, why not let my friend and me go back to our own world? That would free you of our presence, and at the same time nothing could be more for our own good. If you wish, I will even take you up above your highest corridors, and show you the car we came down in—"

The head-lamp of our Oppressor-in-Chief gave a crimson flare.

"So you still persist in your story that you come from

another world?" he demanded. "How often is it necessary to tell you that science has proved there is no other world?"

Perceiving that nothing was to be gained from this line of appeal, I decided to take a different track.

"Then even if we stay in your own land," I entreated, "why cannot we remain as now? We would try our best to learn your laws, and to respect and obey—"

"By the dullness of your heads, what occupation would you pursue?" thundered the Neuter. "How do you think that men without lamps would prosper? Is there any occupation that they could follow in all the million and one corridors of the universe? Could they be engaged in the mines, where head-lamps are necessary to show the way? Or in the factories, which are often without light of their own? Or in the offices of government, which are usually in darkness? No, there is nothing, nothing that they could do. They would remain unemployed. And you know what happens to unemployed men?"

"No, great Lords, I do not know."

"Then let me inform you! There is an ancient statute, dating from remotest times—back from the Sequon 1948— which disposes of the unemployed in a simple and logical fashion. Fortunately, there have been no unemployed for ages; but the statute still exists. Since jobless persons are afflictions to themselves and burdens to society, our ancestors decided that, for humanitarian reasons, it would be well to order them all to report to the authorities, who would have them painlessly and inexpensively asphyxiated. Thus the problem was settled in a way to please economists as well as the more sentimental-minded citizens. It is perfectly possible for you, therefore, if you should prefer that fate—"

Interrupting with an angry gesture, I hastily disclaimed any such preferences.

"Well, at least I am glad you can see the way of reason,"

approved the judge. "The surgical method is of course the best. You will thank us—yes, how you will thank us some day when you are both useful citizens, with newly sprouting head-lamps!"

"Sprouting head-lamps?" I exclaimed. With a vehemence, a paroxysm of anger I had not expected of myself, I stepped toward our judges and waved a threatening fist. "Sprouting head-lamps? By the powers above! I warn you—I warn you not to perform the operation! I will take vengeance—on my honor as an earth man, I will take vengeance if you insist!"

I do not know, nor did I know at the time, what impulse other than madness made me utter these words; and I certainly did not anticipate, as I sank quivering into my seat, the subtle advantage the threat was to give me in days to come. For a babbling laughter sounded from the audience, and hundreds of head-lamps were lighted with an amused lavender; while the Neuters, contemptuous of my outburst, lost no time in deciding that, within fifteen days, Stark and I should undergo the brain operations.

CHAPTER EIGHTEEN
The Beginning of the Scourge

UPON THE conclusion of the trial, Stark and I were returned to our prison, where we were guarded as before by the six-legged monster with the crocodile teeth. There being no possibility of escape, we could do little except to mope in our room with oaths and curses, trying to console one another, while faced with the certainty of speedy execution.

Meantime, as if to keep us from forgetting our impending fate, we received frequent visits from the surgeon who was to perform the operation, as well as from his assistants, all of whom were Neuters with exceptionally long fingers and an exceptionally cold green light in their eyes. Almost like oxen being fattened for the slaughter, we received regular attention, and had our health tested by every device of Plutonian medicine, in order that we might be in condition when the time for the ordeal arrived. If any consolation came to us during those wretched hours, it was in the trouble we gave our captors. Our heart-beat impressed them as abnormally fast, and they debated using injections to retard it—since twenty a minute was considered normal on their planet. Our skin temperature struck them as unbelievably high, and they had to consult their instruments time after time before being convinced—they thought we were suffering from a raging fever, for the normal temperature of a Plutonian—as registered by our thermometers—would be about eighty-eight degrees Fahrenheit.

However, this was not the worst of their difficulties. They

would occupy themselves endlessly in making charts and maps of our heads; they would measure each curve and protuberance; they would take photographs with some machine resembling our X-ray but capable of representing the very convolutions of the brain. The numerous pictures produced by these instruments were searched eagerly for traces of our Superlampular Glands, which, of course, could not be located. But did that deter the physicians from the contemplated operation? Far from it. "See how badly you need medical attention," the Head Surgeon exclaimed, after his eleventh failure to detect any sign of our Superlampular Glands. "Your organs have actually become invisible through disuse. Fortunate for you that we will stimulate them before they disappear entirely."

Stark and I were now being supervised like children being controlled by arrogant adults. One day, for example, in the course of inspecting our clothes while we disrobed for the examinations, the surgeon chanced to catch sight of the gold and precious stones I had secured in the Afflicted Regions. "What are you doing with this trash?" he exclaimed, highly annoyed; and forthwith he flung all my treasures into a receptacle marked "Waste," from which, alas, I was never able to recover them. On another occasion, when Stark and I had determined on a hunger strike, he frustrated our efforts by having us bound and supplying us with nourishment through hypodermic injections. However, most of all he angered us by his refusal to let us see Zandaye, of whom we had not caught sight since the time of her condemnation, and who was the only person on this planet whose presence could have brought us some consolation. Indeed, we did not even receive any word of Zandaye, other than the most indefinite assurances: "Have no fear; she is all right. She is being taken care of... It is part of her punishment not to be allowed to confer again with her partners in crime."

And yet fate, whose method is to burrow like the mole, was already scheming to make our remaining days on Pluto quite different and somewhat brighter than we had anticipated.

Slowly, slowly, but with a speed that seemed excessive, our hours of grace were slipping away. Already half of the allotted time, more than half of the allotted time had passed; less than a week, by earthly reckoning, was left to us—when fortune began to play her antics, and a gleam of hope issued from an unlocked-for direction.

One day, when the Head Surgeon came as usual to examine us, I noticed that from time to time his fingers would feel uneasily at his neck and throat, which seemed slightly swollen. However, neither Stark nor I were particularly interested until, on the following day, we observed that three of the assistants likewise had slight swellings in the same region; while the Head Surgeon had suddenly become fantastic and grotesque of appearance. His neck, formerly of swan-like thinness, had expanded to four times its former size! His lower jaw, which had grown like a lump of dough, was a mere caricature of its original self. It was easy enough, of course, for us to see what was the matter; he had a bad case of the mumps!

Stark and I, naturally, smiled a little at his plight; I will not say that we did not feel a malicious glee. But not until we heard the Surgeon and his assistants discussing the malady did we realize the possible meaning of the blow.

"I cannot imagine what it may be," he said, while tenderly feeling the swollen parts. "By my lamp—but it is painful! I have consulted the books; nothing like it has ever been recorded before."

"No, nothing at all like it," acknowledged one of the others, with a puzzled scowl. "It is doubtless an abscess due to a dental infection. I should advise you to have some teeth pulled immediately."

"No, not by all my fingers," opined a third, reflectively. "For my part, I should say it was due to some gastronomical condition. My own recommendation is that you be careful about your food for the next eight or ten days. Eat little or nothing, and preferably go on a liquid diet."

"By no means, by no means," disagreed a fourth, sharply.

"A sufficiency of food, according to all authorities, is the first necessity in such a case. It is clearly a nervous condition, brought on by overwork and fatigue, which have induced an irritation of the membro-spinal nerve. My suggestion is freedom from worry, and rest, accompanied, if possible, by a change of scenery…"

Overhearing this conversation, Stark and I could not help laughing a little to ourselves. "Why, it seems they've never had any mumps before on Pluto," my companion whispered to me, after the first second of bewilderment; and it was not difficult to come to the conclusion. "Heavens—they must have caught it from us. We must have brought the germs here with us, on our bodies or clothing."

"Lucky we're immune ourselves. Remember, we both had the darned thing when we were ten-year-olds…" I exclaimed. "They must have taken it because of their close contact with us during the medical examinations."

At this thought, we had our first happy moment since our trial; for destiny, it seemed to us, was avenging us for the wrongs we had suffered.

Yet the vengeance was only at its beginning. Next day, the Head Surgeon did not present himself at all; but three of his assistants all had faces like balloons, while three others displayed small swellings that seemed to hold excellent promise. The examination that morning was very brief; and from the way our visitors rubbed their faces and occasionally sighed and groaned, it was apparent that none of them were in too comfortable a state...

After another day, all our attendants alike exhibited faces swollen to fantastic lumps. The chin of one was muffled in bandages; a second was covered with long strips and bands of a substance like court plaster; a third had applied some oily unguent to the afflicted parts; a fourth had tried ice, and a fifth had attempted treatment by means of red-hot cloths; while all alike complained of their plight incessantly, asking each other what the disease might be and whether it were likely to prove fatal. Most of them, after a long consultation, seemed in favor of removing the trouble by operating; but their plans, apparently, came to nothing, for while all were willing to undertake incisions upon their fellows, none would consent to be the subject of the experiment. It amused Stark and me to observe that, while they did not hesitate to hold their debates in our presence, they paid no heed at all to us, and much less thought of consulting us—although we might have told them more than a little about the mysterious malady.

It is fortunate that we did not enlighten them, for we would have abandoned a powerful weapon. But that is to anticipate; Stark and I still did not realize that destiny had done more than to take an irrelevant revenge upon our foes. As yet we were not able to perceive any loophole of escape; we still expected that the knives would take their toll; for time still continued to slip past, and the fateful operation was scheduled to occur within sixty hours.

Being shut off from the world in our single guarded room, we knew nothing of the events agitating the rest of the planet. But after another day or two—when only twenty hours remained of our allotted span of life—sudden realization was to burst upon us. One of our attendants, perhaps rendered careless by a bad case of the mumps, chanced to leave a copy of the *Daily Neuter* in our prison; and Stark and I seized the paper and scanned the contents with as much interest as was possible for men who have only one day more to live.

What was our surprise when we found the whole front page devoted to one subject...

MYSTERIOUS PLAGUE SWEEPS THE WORLD

We read in headlines and more. *Scientists Still Unable to Check Ravages.* And, following this announcement, we saw an article in large type:

The mysterious plague which has been sweeping the world for several days still rages unabated. It seems to be spreading in wide circles from a central focus, and each hour thousands of new sufferers are being listed by the Supervisor of Public Health. The symptoms, which are unparalleled in medical records, are featured by a violent and painful swelling in the region of the neck and chin, which in some instances grow to several times their normal size. Worst of all, in severe cases the head-lamps have been affected, and have been unable to shed beams of normal brilliancy. It is not known how many of the sufferers will recover, but already more than three hundred deaths have occurred, of which over half have been among Neuters. Millions not yet stricken are fleeing in a panic from the affected regions, bringing business to a standstill and threatening a tie up of scientific activity, of transportation, and of the Synthetic Food Factories. However, no method has yet been discovered for checking the epidemic.

The most singular feature of the pestilence is that it has occurred simultaneously among so many people, almost as though one had conveyed it to another—a method of transmission which, according to physicians, is impossible. In their efforts to explain the incredible, some persons say that the victims unconsciously set up vicious waves in the air, which impinge upon the bodies of their neighbors and affect them with the malady. Still others claim that the sufferers throw off base humors, which settling on the skins of their friends, cause the disease to sprout from fungus-like spores. Others, again—being of a devout turn of mind—contend that our people have gone so far in the way of iniquity that the Creator is issuing a judgment upon them…

But a still more striking theory is rapidly gaining credence in some quarters. It is pointed out that the plague originated in the vicinity of the two man-like creatures, known as the Lampless Ones, who came from no one can say where, and whose ways are monstrous and inexplicable. It is also pointed out that one of these creatures, upon being promised an operation which would cause his lamp to grow, was so far from appreciating the preferred benefaction that he fell into a fit of anger, and made fiery promises of vengeance. Of course, no one at first took such ravings seriously; but observers are now asking whether it was by a mere coincidence that the Head Surgeon, who was to have performed the operation, was the first to be stricken, while his assistants followed in short order. Is it not possible, investigators are asking, that the Lampless Ones deliberately infected the Head Surgeon with some secret poison which the victim would communicate unknowingly to whomever he might touch? In that case, would there be any way of preventing the spread of the pestilence without the aid of the Lampless Ones?"

It is needless to state that this article was a revelation to Stark and myself. With staring eyes, we re-read the account, wondering whether we could have misconstrued the meaning; then, while not yet realizing fully the possibilities, we turned to one another as exultantly as dying men who see an unexpected hope.

"So…" exclaimed Stark, "it's not only that the mumps were never known in this world before, it's that no contagious disease was ever known."

"Apparently not," I concurred. "Evidently bacteria have never been discovered here."

"Well, surely, it's not up to us to educate the people," he continued, brushing back the newly sprouting mat of hair that was overrunning his glass head-lamp. "Our best course will be to pretend we did it all deliberately."

"'Let them think I carried out that threat of mine," I said, taking up the argument. "Let them believe we have some secret power! Let them imagine we can end the plague as easily as we started it. In that case, how can they risk killing us in an operation?"

"Yes, but the operation is such a short distance away," groaned Stark. "We'll have to work fast—terribly fast!"

For the next hour, we might have been observed in a sly, whispered conversation. Sometimes we were absorbed with a seriousness that brought the wrinkles to our brows; sometimes we might have been noticed to chuckle furtively; occasionally we sat beaming at one another with radiant hopefulness… And the result of our conference was a plot that we began to carry out at the first opportunity.

That opportunity arrived with the entry of two attendants—equipped with machines for registering our blood pressure and heartbeat for the last time before the operation. We observed that their faces were already swollen with incipient cases of the mumps; and we did not fail to take advantage of that fact.

"Put down your instruments," I surprised them by directing, in a calm but determined voice. "You are not to take any measurements today. We will not allow the operation to be performed. If you so much as touch us—yes, so much as let your hands rest on ours—we will inject a venom into your veins. As a result, you will die in agony of the disease, which is called—"

"Which is called the Bloated Neck," finished Stark for me, on an inspiration.

The attendants stared at us with head-lamps of a sudden yellow, but neither of them approached.

"We have produced the disease," I proceeded. "We alone can end it. It is our protest against the operations that you propose to perform. If you still perform them, then your world will never be able to free itself from the pestilence."

The Plutonians stood peering at us with small mouths agape; second by second their head-lamps seemed to burn to a deeper yellow.

"But, Lampless Ones—honored Lampless Ones," one of them faltered, with a respect he had never displayed before, "it is not we that are to blame. We are acting under orders. The Head Surgeon has instructed us—"

"Then we must speak with the Head Surgeon," I demanded. "Tell him to come here. We must see him at once…"

"Very well—very well, honored Lampless Ones," conceded the attendant. "But do you not know how hard it is for anyone to get speech with the Head Surgeon?"

Even as he spoke, he grasped the arm of his fellow, with whom he began to retreat from the room as rapidly as if it had been infested with serpents.

Stark and I had not long to wait for the next act in the drama. Within twenty minutes we heard hasty footsteps from without, and several Neuters entered, among them the Head Surgeon.

He was looking unusually pale and wan even for a Plutonian, and the bulges on his chin and neck showed that he was still far from having recovered from the mumps.

"What is this nonsense I hear?" he burst forth, as he strode into the room; and had his voice not indicated anger, the red glow on his head would have amply suggested it. "By my lamp—I am told you refuse to prepare for the operation!"

"You are told correctly," I said. "We propose to remain without head-lights."

The Surgeon uttered something that may have been a curse. However, not being sufficiently versed in Plutonian profanity, I cannot say positively.

"And why, pray, this presumption?" he demanded, in tones tinged with irony. "Do you think you will make better citizens if you cannot find your way in the dark?"

"Do you think you will make a better citizen if you go about with the Bloated Neck?" I retorted.

Our adversary stared at us with eyes that were little more than two penetrating points of greenish fire.

"I do not understand what that has to do with the operations," he declared, crisply.

As briefly as I could, I repeated what I had already said to the attendant, as to the cause of the Bloated Neck and its probable duration.

He listened with angry flares of his head-lamp, but without any evidence of surprise.

"Well, so that is what you say?" he challenged, when I had finished. "But am I to believe it? What proof have you that you are really responsible for the disease?"

"Did I not threaten to take vengeance if you insisted on the operation?" I flung back, fiercely.

"And have you observed," added Stark, "that neither my friend or I have taken the Swollen Neck? How does that happen, when everyone else around us has been stricken?"

A long silence followed this question, and I saw that we had scored. The Head Surgeon turned to his fellows, and they nodded to him significantly... "Yes, how does it happen that the Lampless Ones have not taken the disease?" they whispered, but he made no response.

"You shall see that we never shall take the disease," I proceeded. "You shall also see that, if you deal with us rightly, we can show you how to treat the trouble, so that in time it will disappear from your world. Otherwise, there will be no relief."

Another long silence followed. The Head Surgeon conferred in whispers with his companions, so that we could catch only occasional words and phrases, such as "Public danger," "Wrong to take any chances," and "Peril to our lamps."

At last the Surgeon turned to us abruptly and demanded, "Well, just what do you want us to do?"

"Call off the operations…" Stark and I returned, in one voice.

He screwed up his thin lips solemnly, and tenderly stroked the swollen parts of his neck.

"That is impossible," he announced. "It would require the sanction of the Head Neuter and the Governing Council, who control the world's affairs, and who have been informed of the approaching operations and inscribed them on the Books of State. To be sure, if you request it, we might make an appeal.

"How long would that require?"

The Surgeon hesitated. "Well, with luck," he finally ventured, "we might have our answer within three days."

Stark and I groaned, "But by that time the operations would be over!"

"To be sure," nodded the Surgeon. "But at least you would have the satisfaction of knowing whether they were legally justified."

"What if the operations were to be postponed?" Stark demanded. "Would that not be legal?"

"No, by my lamp, strictly illegal."

"Strictly illegal!" repeated several decisive voices.

"Then long may the Bloated Neck remain among you," I flared.

Another long silence ensued, followed by a second whispered conference among the Neuters, whose head-lamps displayed many a telltale yellow spark.

Then once more the Head Surgeon turned to us, and, with a brighter expression on his face, declared:

"My assistants and I think we have found a way. While it is illegal and rightly punishable, as we have stated, to postpone an operation deliberately, it is not illegal or punishable in the least to postpone it unintentionally. So what if my colleagues and I should find that we were too severely stricken by the new disease to wield a knife? In that way we might delay the operation for several days, and meanwhile your appeal might be heard by the Head Neuter and his council. Would that satisfy you?"

"Perfectly," Stark and I acknowledged, delight written across our faces.

However, when I stepped forward to seize the Surgeon's hand in token of appreciation, he started back as if I intended to strike him. All his kinsmen shrank from contact with me as though I had been a leper; while the spectacle they made as they hastily retreated from the room reminded me of a fireworks exhibition in yellow.

PART
SIX

CHAPTER NINETEEN
The Hall of the Rose-Red Light

INSTEAD OF being taken to the operating room on the next morning, Stark and I received orders to appear before the Head Neuter.

In the company of several attendants, all of whom displayed well developed cases of the Bloated Neck and kept us at as great a distance as though we were "untouchables," we were escorted hundreds of miles on an expedition of several hours. During the course of our journey, we made some interesting observations, chiefly to the effect that the epidemic had spread far more thoroughly than we had guessed. Here and there we passed galleries crowded with lamp-heads, of whom the great majority exhibited bulging necks and chins, while many were bandaged with heavy cloths, and not a few were groaning and wailing. All ages alike were affected, from tottering old Neuters to children who reached but little above my knees. All seemed to blame us as for their affliction. They would point to us with jeers and cries, and in some cases, when their head-lamps were swollen and burned but poorly, they would indicate those organs with pitiful lamentations and deluge us with curses.

Now and then we were even threatened with physical violence, and were only saved by the popular dread of contact with us. However, we were fortunate when a group of half-grown urchins conceived the idea of attacking us with stones. Despite the protests of our attendants, who, we could see, secretly sympathized with the assailants, we were the targets of a savage bombardment, and had a lively time dodging showers of rocks, some of them as big as our fists. Only when we proved ourselves capable of seizing the rocks and hurling them back with damaging force did the assault show signs of relaxing; and, even so, we were lucky to escape without serious injury. Yet we suffered only one casualty. A heavy stone—the last one flung by our enemies—caught me on what remained of my crystal head-lamp, shattering it to fragments and momentarily stunning me. A minute later, we had escaped through a little door into a side-gallery.

Most of our trip, fortunately, was accomplished upon movable platforms that took us far from the rabble; and so the battle was not renewed, although we realized that henceforth we would live on Pluto not only as aliens, but as aliens on enemy soil.

Consequently, we were relieved when our journey was over. Passing through a great triangular doorway surmounted by the sign, "Head Neuter," we were bidden to wait in an octagonal room with translucent walls of some substance like amber. "His Ruling Eminence is engaged in a conference just now," we were informed. "But if you will wait in the anteroom, he will see you when he is at leisure."

Having no choice, we took seats on the floor, while our attendants ranged themselves near the doorway as if to preclude our escape. Minute after minute went by, during which we did nothing but shift uneasily from place to place and beat time upon our knees. Then, when my impatience had bidden me to arise and begin pacing the floor, I heard the sound of voices from an inner room, a door swung open, and a weeping woman with a yellow head-light and bandaged face emerged.

At first, in my astonishment, I failed to recognize her. But it was only a moment before I had cried out, in tune with Stark, "Zandaye...Zandaye!"

Startled, she looked up with swollen, red-lidded eyes, and with an exclamation of surprise and joy ran to us, giving one hand impulsively to each.

"Zandaye!" we called out together. "What—what are you doing here?"

She glanced about her furtively, as if to make sure that none of the attendants were overhearing. Then, in whispers she confided, "Oh, my friends, my friends. The Head Neuter has just called me to see him. By my lamp, but we have had a long conference. It was all about you! He—he threatens—such penalties—unless I tell him all I know. He thinks that I, having been with you so long, know how you caused this—this horrible disease. You see, I am stricken with it myself. I told him you had not caused it at all, but he would not believe me…"

"You should not have told him that, Zandaye," I remonstrated; and then, seeing her bewildered look, stopped suddenly short.

"Never mind, Zandaye," promised Stark, while bravely she tried to dry away the last trace of her tears, "we will protect you. We will speak to the Head Neuter—"

It was at this point that a voice thundered from the unseen: "His Ruling Eminence, the Head Neuter, is in waiting, along with Their Distinguished Excellencies, the Governing Council. The two Larnpless Ones will step forward, following the green arrow into the Audience Chamber."

As these words died out, half of the wall to our right slid open, revealing a winding gallery whose existence we had not suspected. Upon the floor a flaming green arrow was visible; and this we followed hastily, after bidding a hurried farewell to Zandaye, who watched us with dismal eyes as we nodded and slipped from view.

After threading our way through intricate passages in

which we would have been lost had it not been for the green arrow, Stark and I climbed a long flight of stairs and emerged into a hall suffused with an eerie rose-red light. We were wondering whether, after all, we had not gone astray, when a voice from the invisible exclaimed, "You will now lift your left hands three times in token of respect for His Ruling Eminence, the Head Neuter, and Their Distinguished Excellencies, the Governing Council."

As we performed the required ceremony, we noticed a queer-looking pyramidal marble stand, about twelve or fifteen feet high, which towered near one end of the hall. At its apex sat a being with a particularly brilliant head-lamp and a head three times the ordinary size; just beneath him stared several empty benches; while on seats ranged at different heights along the pyramid sat six or eight big-headed Neuters, who, I must admit, did not present a particularly dignified appearance. Indeed, several of them were nodding and tossing in sleep, while all their faces alike displayed huge unsightly lumps and swellings. The personage on the highest seat, alone of all the group, had not contracted the Bloated Neck; and it impressed me at once that he looked like a ruler, as, suffused in a rosy glow, and clad only in the long, diaphanous streamers that hung from his head-lamp, he returned our salutation by raising his left hand twice, and then solemnly motioned us to approach.

Was it surprising that our hearts leapt as we drew near this personage who held our fate in his hands? True, he was not strikingly different to the outer eye from hundreds of Plutionans; but the inner eye, perceiving the power that he wielded, translated that power at once into magnificence. We could not have shuddered more violently had we been summoned to the throne of great Jove himself.

"Greetings, Lampless Ones!" he boomed, when at last we stood beneath him, staring up somewhat as a small dog stares at its master, "I have called you here today on a most serious matter. You may judge of its importance when I tell you that, in order to see you, I had to postpone a meeting of the Inter-Neuter Political League, which is entrusted with the duty of choosing the candidates for both sides in our elections. What was even more regrettable, I had to miss the Three Hundredth Sequonal meeting of the Society to Reform the Afflicted Regions, of which I am an Honorary Vice Secretary. Well, duty before pleasure is the Neuter motto. And so I have sent for you, since I find my subordinates too panic-stricken to perform a simple operation upon your heads. This was the proposed date of the operation, was it not?"

We both nodded.

"I thought so. Then, by my lamp, let us get to the point."

Suddenly his manner became brisk, business-like; he sat up almost with military erectness; his voice assumed such thunder and volume that several of his associates, aroused from their slumbers, stirred and rubbed their eyes sleepily before dozing off—again.

"As you say," he continued, "the operation was to have been performed today. Assuredly, it should have been performed, for your crimes and blunders can only be explained by the emotional blankness and the mental derangements due to the lack of a lamp. But now comes the most serious charge of all. It is said you have deliberately spread a horrible scourge, which swells the neck and sometimes dims the head-lamp. If this is true, then it is doubtful whether an operation would cure you; indeed, it might be best to submit you to the process of Fiery Annihilation—a punishment rarely applied, but never known to fail. However, I do not believe you guilty of spreading the disease. I attribute the charge to the ignorance, the credulity, and the prejudice of the masses. Besides, one of your friends, whom I have just interviewed, assures me that you are not responsible. But before dismissing the case and sending you back to the operating room, I should like to hear from your own lips a denial of the accusations…"

The Head Neuter brought seven long fingers down upon his bare knee with a slap that disturbed the Governing Council once more in their slumbers. Then, folding his arms in an attitude of waiting, he sat peering down at us for several long embarrassing seconds, until Stark, in a wavering voice, made bold to speak:

"I am sorry, Your Ruling Eminence, but who am I to combat the truth? My friend and I, being men of honor, will not deny the accusations."

The Head Neuter shot far forward in his seat, and his great greenish eyes flashed and sparkled.

"By your lampless skulls!" he roared. "Then you mean to say you are guilty—guilty of the most monstrous crimes?"

"We are responsible," testified Stark, with increasing assurance, "for starting and spreading the disease known as the Bloated Neck."

Suddenly the seven fingers of the Neuter's powerful right hand were clenched, and drove forward with the force of a projectile.

"This is preposterous!" he bellowed. "You do not know what you say. Why, have you even considered the penalty? You lay yourselves open to the doom of Fiery Annihilation. And, by the holy head-lamp of my father, that is what you will suffer—yes, that is what you will suffer unless it be proved you are speaking mere words…"

"I am not speaking mere words," insisted Stark.

"No, Your Ruling Eminence," I verified, "he is not speaking mere words."

"Then Fiery Annihilation will be the reward of you both."

"I don't think so," Stark denied, while several members of the Governing Council, newly aroused, yawned and stared at him with their first show of interest. "You will not annihilate the only men who know how to free you from the Bloated Neck."

"How do I know you can free us from the Bloated Neck?"

"If we spread pestilence, we can also relieve it," my friend asserted. "Without us, you cannot save yourselves."

"Besides," I added, on an inspiration, "if you do not cure the disease, it will grow worse by its very nature. Some of your people, to be sure, will recover, but they will fall victim to it again and again. After a while, it will disfigure most of you, and injure or destroy your head-lamps."

The Head Neuter groaned. Several members of the Governing Council did likewise, and a yellow glitter came into their lamps. As if by instinct, their leader felt for his luminary before, in a wrathful voice, he continued:

"What is that you say? What diabolical threat is this you make? Truly, Lampless Ones, as some of our scientists have testified, you cannot be even half-human—otherwise, how could you dream of such criminal speech? Have you thought of the defenseless millions of Neuters and children? But no—by the brilliance of my head-light—you cannot think at all. Everything that you say is an idle threat..."

Into Stark's eyes there had come a sudden ironic twinkling.

"Idle threat?" he repeated, in low vibrant tones. "Perhaps you will say so when, for sequons and sequons to come, you will see millions groaning and distorted with the Bloated Neck. But maybe you would like a little proof? If you see that I can cause the Bloated Neck, will you be convinced that I can cure it?"

"Yes, by my lamp, I will be convinced..." thundered the Head Neuter, swinging his long lithe body so far forward that I feared he would topple out of his seat and come tumbling down upon us. "But how, in the name of all bright-shining heads, can you cause the disease?"

"That I will gladly show," Stark proceeded, while I wondered what trickery he could be planning. "It will, however, be necessary for you to perform a few simple acts, and after that you must wait a few days. If you will consent to this much—"

"I will consent to anything reasonable," vowed the Head Neuter; but his greenish eyes had an incredulous gleam. "What is it that you propose?"

"First of all, summon a few people who have not had the Bloated Neck. Five or six will be enough."

The Head Neuter scowled. "Five or six who have not had the Bloated Neck will be difficult to find," he ruminated. "A hasty census has shown that not one in a thousand has escaped, I myself have been one of the fortunate few—which doubtless is because the Powers Above wish to protect me, whom the people need to lead them... However, since you desire to show that you can cause the disease, it seems reasonable to begin on those who have never had it. If you will therefore retire for a while, I will send out scouts to find some persons who have escaped. With luck, you will be called back within a few hours."

The Head Neuter lifted his left hand in token of our dismissal, and the members of the Governing Council yawned and settled back to sleep once more. Stark and I, passing out through a door that opened automatically to receive us, followed a red arrow through a long passageway to the anteroom where we had waited before.

At the first opportunity, I whispered a pertinent question, and Stark chuckled, and whispered back something that made me also chuckle. "Do you think it will work?" he concluded, with an expressive gleam in his great blue eyes.

"Don't see how it can fail," I returned; and, chuckling once more, I congratulated my friend on an ingenious plan.

It was only about two hours later when a voice from the invisible roared the announcement that His Ruling Eminence, the Head Neuter, again desired to see us.

Accordingly, we wasted no time about following the green arrow in the company of several attendants, and within a few minutes stood again in the rose-hued hall beneath the pyramidal throne.

"Well, Lampless Ones," bawled the Head Neuter, after we had performed the expected ceremony with our left hands, "I have secured six persons unaffected by the Bloated Neck. Shall I call them?"

"If you please, Your Ruling Eminence," acquiesced Stark. And the Head Neuter signaled to an attendant, who signaled to another attendant, who signaled to a third attendant; following which a door slipped open, and six ordinary-looking Plutonians, untouched by disease, entered the hall with head-lamps of an intense yellow.

"Your Ruling Eminence, I found these individuals only after great difficulty," testified one of the helpers. "None of them wished to come, but I assured them that the welfare of the State may depend on their presence."

"So it may," acknowledged the Head Neuter. "And now, Lampless Ones, will you advise me what to do next?"

"Certainly, Your Ruling Eminence," asserted Stark. "Will you now order a bowl of any kind of liquid food, with a tube to drink from?"

The head-lamp of the Neuter showed a sudden crimson. His eyes burned with an intense, baleful green. "Lampless Ones," he cried, bringing his great fist down angrily upon his knee, "I have told you I will listen to any reasonable request—but I will not be made sport of…"

"If Your Ruling Eminence will only do as I say, he will find my request to be most reasonable," promised Stark. "What harm can there be in getting a small bowl of food?"

"What harm, indeed?" echoed one of the members of the Governing Council, who, at the mention of food, showed the first real interest he had yet manifested.

With snarling reluctance, the Head Neuter assented, "Very well, then. But I warn you—as I value my lamp. Fiery Annihilation will not be the worst you have to fear if you are taking my good nature in vain."

A few minutes later, a bowl of a soup-like fluid was brought in, along with one of the tubes by means of which the Plutonians were accustomed to eating.

At the sight of these objects, the Governing Council sat up alertly. The Head Neuter sarcastically barked, "All right, Lampless Ones…here is your dinner. Now what do you propose to do? Eat it?"

"By no means," denied Stark. "Watch carefully, everyone." And he reached down, muttered to me in English, "We've got to do this well—our last chance depends on it." Then he waved his hands before the bowl as if to hypnotize it, and blew upon it solemnly and ceremoniously three times; after which he ostentatiously took a sip of the food.

A silence had fallen upon the assemblage; all looked on with head-lamps that had flashed to an orange of surprise.

"And now," Your Ruling Eminence," added Stark, "I have one or two simple requests still to make. I wonder, will one of the Distinguished Excellencies be so good as to take a sip of this food?"

"By my lamp, why not?" cried the Head Neuter, with a scowl of vast disapproval. "When did I ever dictate what the Distinguished Excellencies may eat?"

"Personally, I should like to oblige the Lampless Ones," volunteered one of the Governing Council, whose face was bulging from a particularly severe attack of the mumps. And, without further ceremony, he reached down, took the tube between his lips, and drained a long draught.

"Now," continued Stark, while the Head Neuter still scowled down upon us, "will one of the persons without the Bloated Neck take a sip?"

Since the Head Neuter did not positively forbid, the tube was passed to one of the newcomers, who, never suspecting our plot—since nothing was known on Pluto regarding contagious diseases or their transmission—took a sip without asking that the tube be washed or even wiped.

Then once more a member of the Governing Council was asked to drink; then one of the persons without the Bloated Neck, and so again and again until the entire half dozen had had every chance to be infected:

"Now if Your Ruling Eminence will wait about six or seven days," declared Stark, after the ceremonies were all over, "you will find that all the persons you have called here today have been taken with the Bloated Neck."

The Head Neuter's reply was an incredulous smile, accompanied by a lavender flash.

"Lampless Ones," he mocked, "I thought you would try to show us a real trick. I thought you would not do something utterly silly. How can a man take the Bloated Neck simply by tasting everyday food? Here…it is all so senseless I will show you how little there is to it! I will taste the food myself!"

To our shocked surprise, the Head Neuter ordered the bowl to be brought up to him, whereupon he tasted the food by means of the tube used by all the others.

"Now, Lampless Ones," he concluded, "this will prove how foolish you have been. I will wait seven days; then, if the Bloated Neck be not found among those of us who did not have it before, that will be proof that you are imposters and did not cause the disease. In that case, I swear, by the brilliance of my lamp, I will order the physicians immediately to perform the operations to give you the light…"

Once more the Head Neuter laughed a skeptical laugh; and then beckoned to the attendants to lead us back to prison.

CHAPTER TWENTY
His Ruling Eminence Proclaims

AFTER ANOTHER WEEK in the monotony of our guarded room, Stark and I were again summoned before the Head Neuter.

Our first glimpse of that official, as we entered the rose-hued hall, showed us that not all had gone well with him. He had lost much of his former majesty; his face was swathed in bandages that did not quite conceal the grotesque swellings of the chin and neck; while his head-lamp had swollen to double its normal size and at the same time had been dimmed to half its normal brilliancy.

It is not surprising, accordingly, that he was not in a very good humor; that he called out, "Greetings, Lampless Ones!" in a voice that was like a snarl, and glared at us with morose greenish eyes that looked as if they would like to devour us.

The seats on the pyramidal throne, we observed, were now mostly vacant; only two or three members of the Governing Council were present; while, as if to replace the absentees, several persons were ranged in a semi-circle on the floor beneath the throne. And these we recognized with difficulty as the objects of Stark's experiment. But how changed they were—all were nursing enormous bulging chins and cheeks.

"You see, Lampless Ones," growled the Head Neuter, when we had come to a respectful halt beneath him, "you see what you have done. Evil piled on evil. By the light of my head—what do you mean by infecting all these poor people with this loathsome disease? Yes, and what do you mean by giving it to me—me, on whom the burden of the whole world rests? Do you not realize what you have done? One who attacks the person of the Head of the State is guilty of an attack on the State itself—and an attack on the State is punished by a doom a thousand times worse than Fiery Annihilation..."

Stark and I, exchanging meaningful glances, were beginning to lose the jubilation we had felt at the success of our plan.

"The person of the Head of the State is sacred," continued the Neuter, after pausing long enough to rub his swollen face tenderly. "You do not know how this accursed disease hurts! I have not decided what penalty to order, Lampless Ones, but you will not go free with a mere operation. No operation could cure depravity such as yours."

"Your Ruling Eminence," pleaded Stark, "are you not forgetting the experiment you consented to have me perform? I promised to infect six persons with the Bloated Neck, and have I not done so? But I did not intend to include you. It was you yourself, remember, who drank from the common bowl without consulting me—"

"Who are you, that I have to consult you?" shouted the Head Neuter, in a strained and husky voice. '

"But if Your Ruling Eminence had consulted me, you would not now have the Bloated Neck," continued Stark, unperturbed, "and if you will still consult me, you will be cured of the disease, and all your people will be cured. Just as my friend and I have started the pestilence, so we can end it."

"How?" demanded the Head Neuter, poking his long thin body forward like a leaning tower. "By my lamp, how can you end it?"

"That is what I want to show. After making the cure, I will explain my method. However, first I must be free to act.

I must have your word of honor as Head Neuter that my friend and I will not be operated on or punished."

"By all the powers of darkness, you have your impudence," muttered the Head Neuter. "Not operated on or punished? After the crimes you have committed?"

"You have our terms," shrugged Stark.

For a moment, the Head Neuter remained wrapped in a thoughtful silence. His head-lamp, enfeebled by disease, showed a pale red tinged with yellow; his hand felt appraisingly for his swollen face, and he groaned involuntarily as he touched a tender part. Then, still glaring at us with those hostile green eyes, he grumbled:

"Well, by rights, Lampless Ones, both of you should be left to hang in a pit of burning sulfur for a thousand sequons. Such a fate would be less than you deserve. Yet, for the sake of my people, I may forget my personal grievances and treat even with traitors. So you say that you can cure us all of the Bloated Neck, and that the disease will never return?"

"That is what I say, Your Ruling Eminence."

"How long would this take?"

Stark hesitated. "That depends, Your Ruling Eminence, on whether you will carry out a few necessary requests. If so, I can promise that, in seven days, the disease will begin to disappear throughout the land, while after twice seven days there will be no trace of it left."

"And what are the requests that you make?" demanded the Head Neuter.

"They are not many, Your Ruling Eminence, but they are very important. First I ask that, during the next seven days, my friend and I be free to roam anywhere in the world."

"Granted!" snapped the Head Neuter. "Naturally, you must be free to go where you will in order to end the disease. However, in that case someone must be appointed to accompany you."

"Very well, Your Ruling Eminence," assented Stark. "I ask that we travel in the company of one of our former tutors, a female named Zandaye—"

"Zandaye—" interrupted the Head Neuter, with a scowl. "Zandaye Zandippar? Yes, I remember her. A very stout person, is she not, with the oddest red lips and blue eyes? Well, there is something to be said for her. She has already had training enough in Pre-Neuterhood to make a capable guide."

After a moment's hesitation, the Head Neuter signaled to one of the attendants standing in the rear. "Send out a call for Demoted Pre-Neuter Zandaye Zandippar," he shouted a husky command. "At once. Tell her it is my wish."

"Now—one thing more, Your Ruling Eminence," I requested, after the attendant had retired. "Not long ago this Pre-Neuter, Zandaye, was unjustly dishonored, I therefore ask you to free her from disgrace and restore her to Pre-Neuterhood."

The scowl that darkened the face of the Head Neuter reminded me of a thundercloud. One of his great seven-fingered hands waved before me in a storm of anger. "Now Lampless One, what can all that have to do with you?" he demanded. "How can the honor or dishonor of this Zandaye affect the Bloated Neck?"

"Your Ruling Eminence," I pleaded, "need I explain that Zandaye can be of most use to us if she works with an untroubled mind? I assure you, this is indispensable… If you will not consent, we can do nothing about the Bloated Neck."

The Head Neuter groaned, but after a moment's hesitation, during which he glowered at us as if to say that our last moment was at hand, he summoned another attendant, who procured a long sheet of parchment-like paper, on which several sentences were written with a flourish, to be followed by the signature of the Head Neuter.

"We will give her this when she comes," he declared, "and now, Larnpless Ones, you have asked everything you wish?"

"No, Your Ruling Eminence," Stark surprised me by saying. "There is just one trifle more. When my friend and I came among your people, we had some clothes that were not as those worn here. These clothes were taken from us, and we have not seen them since. Unfortunately, I had concealed in them some powders powerful against the Bloated Neck. Therefore if you will but send for these garments—"

"By my lamp," interrupted the Head Neuter, "that will not be easy. After being shipped to our chemical laboratories for analysis, they have been placed behind glass cases in museums, where they are still on exhibition. The directors of the museums will not gladly consent to releasing such curiosities. Is it essential to have them?"

"Absolutely essential."

"Absolutely," I coincided, admiring my friend's forethought. "But after the seven days, we will return them to you."

"Then, as I live, if it must be…it must!" sighed His Ruling Eminence. "But I am not anxious to antagonize the directors of the museums, who are all Neuters of high standing."

Without delay, however, he summoned another attendant, and muttered an order…

At the same time, we were bidden to return to the anteroom; and there for several hours we could do nothing but wait. However, upon being called back into the presence of the Head Neuter, we observed two great fur coats in a rumpled heap on the floor just beneath the Neuter's throne. The fur had been singed or clipped off in a few places, and parts of the collars had been slit, yet apparently the garments had not lost their usefulness.

"Greetings, Lampless Ones," growled His Ruling Eminence, as we performed the required rites with our left hands. "Here are your costumes. Unsightly as they are, may they give you joy and length of sequons. I fear I have made enemies for life of the museum directors—but, by the sooty light of their heads, that can't be helped."

We had hardly finished examining the fur coats when an attendant announced the arrival of Zandaye.

"Tell her to come here at once," directed the Head Neuter. And so, within a few minutes, we had again seen our friend. Her face, we were glad to observe, was no longer bandaged. She seemed almost to have recovered from the mumps. However, her eyes were downcast and when she noticed us it was with a shock of surprise. Her head-lamp showed a deep yellow glow.

"Greetings, Zandaye Zandippar," cried the Head Neuter, after she had performed the salutations with her left hand. "Do not be disturbed at being summoned today. I have good news for you. Rare and undeserved good news. Attendants, will you show her the official proclamation?"

The long parchment-like paper, with the signature of the Head Neuter, was accordingly placed in Zandaye's hands. Her thin form reeled as her eyes raced along the contents; she gave a gasp of incredulous surprise, and might have fallen in a swoon had not two attendants rushed to her assistance.

"Why, I—I— Ruling Eminence, what have I done to earn this?" she faltered. When she was in a condition to speak half coherently, "I—I a Pre-Neuter again! The blessings of ten thousand sequons be upon you. Ruling Emin—"

"Do not bless me," the Head Neuter cut her short. "It was not done of my own desire. Bless the Lampless Ones, who argued your case so well that I could refuse them nothing."

Zandaye turned toward us with a look of such gratitude in her flooded eyes that I felt that all our recent sufferings had not been in vain. Her head-lamp glowed to a lovely blue; her voice trembled as she exclaimed, "By my light, dear friends, you have saved my honor! You have saved my life! Now that the road to Neuterhood is open once more—"

"Come, come," broke in the Head Neuter impatiently. "You can discuss all that after our business is concluded. We must now get down to work again."

Thereupon he informed Zandaye that she was to be our guide for seven days and take us wherever we wished to go.

"Here," he concluded, scribbling a few lines upon a small red card, "this will serve as a passport for the three of you in any gallery or Traveling Platform. It will also entitle you to food and shelter at any of the Neuter Hotels. But your rights will expire in seven days. After that time, I will expect you all back here again. By the power of my lamp, I will have you brought back forcibly if you do not come of your own will. Also, I will expect to find that this dread disease, which you call the Bloated Neck, is everywhere receding."

"Yes, Your Ruling Eminence," promised Stark, "that is what you will find."

"If not—by my fourteen fingers, remember—Fiery Annihilation, or worse!" thundered the Head Neuter.

"We have no fear, Your Ruling Eminence."

"Then you had better make the most of your time. Now be gone..."

We thanked His Ruling Eminence; and after raising our left hands once more in token of respect, Stark and I hastily left in the company of Zandaye and an attendant.

Our last glimpse of the Head Neuter, as we glided from the room, showed him tenderly feeling his swollen neck. "Well, colleagues," he groaned, as he awakened a member of the Governing Council by prodding him with one foot, "suppose we say we've worked enough for today. By my lamp, I'm not feeling any too well, and I think I'll be going home for some rest..."

CHAPTER TWENTY-ONE
The End of It All

AS SOON AS STARK and I were alone with Zandaye, we began to explain our plans. Without unfolding our purpose fully, we asked to be taken to the long ice-coated stairway by which we had descended into the planet. At first Zandaye did not know which stairway we meant, for there were many narrow, deserted tunnels which led up from the Upper or Frigid Corridors, though none of them had been used for ages because of the unbearable cold. But after we had explained that the stairs led into a triangular gallery near a hexagonal court, Zandaye recognized the place; there was only one such gallery in the world, she said, and that was a very, very ancient one, of a style of construction long outmoded.

As it was only a few hours' journey away, we set out at once, using a "Traveling Platform," while both Stark and I exulted to think that escape was so near. There was only one thing to trouble us—what were we to do with Zandaye? Could we not take her with us to earth? What a sensation she would make there! Besides, was there not still a chance that she would marry me? So accustomed had I now become to the peculiarities of Plutonian anatomy that it did not even occur to me that it would seem grotesque to have a wife with a head-lamp and fourteen fingers.

The opportunity to press my suit came when at last we had paused to eat at one of the "Neuter Hotels" and Stark had strolled off by himself to observe a peculiar crystalline gallery.

Her head-lamp showed an orange of surprise when I hastily put the question.

"Why, dear friend of mine," she exclaimed, giving me the same answer as once before, "you know that is impossible. I—I am to become a Neuter."

"But, Zandaye, if you leave this world with me it will not matter whether you are to become a Neuter or not. Think, will it not be wonderful to go far away—"

"No, no, it is impossible!" she cut me short, a wistful light in her glistening blue eyes. "Impossible! I am to become a Neuter; I cannot forsake my duties. Oh, my friend, if you wanted me to go with you, why did you have me restored to Pre-Neuterhood?"

"Why? Because you were so unhappy, Zandaye." And then, as a sudden light burst upon me, "Tell me—if your rank had not been restored—would you—would you then, maybe—"

She hung her head, and her lamp showed a deep blue radiance.

As realization shot over me, I groaned to think that in my very zeal to win her I had lost her forever.

Even so, I might still have pleaded had it not been for Stark's sudden return. In his company, we resumed our journey; yet within a few minutes he had found a pretext to go roaming away with her down a side-corridor while I remained waiting alone. What transpired during the interval I do not know, but they were both gone for many minutes, and when they returned, Stark looked exceedingly solemn, while Zandaye's eyes were tearful and red...

Only an hour later, we entered the triangular gallery that I had witnessed some of our first adventures on the planet. It was like our previous visit: the long empty spaces, the branching side-corridors, and the all-suffusing radiance proceeding from no visible source in the granite walls. To find the point of our original descent was less easy, and several hours were occupied in the task, while we ranged back and forth for miles…until at last we found the hexagonal court, and, a few minutes later, made out a remembered circular opening in the roof.

Now we laid our plans completely before Zandaye. Until this moment, she had not known that we were to escape at this particular point. And how her face was distorted with horror, how her head-lamp glared and flickered with yellow flashes when we adjusted our fur coats and told her that we expected to climb into the stairway above the triangular gallery!

"By my father's lamp—you can't do that!" she gasped, in a voice of terror. "You can't! It's forbidden! And what of me, left here alone—"

"What of you?" I echoed, with a sudden sickening sensation. "Yes, what of you, Zandaye?"

All at once it had come to me that our escape was not practicable. If we got away, would Zandaye not have to bear the brunt? Would the Head Neuter not vent his wrath on her? No—we must remain, though we might face Fiery Annihilation.

The same thought must have come simultaneously to Stark. "Yes, it is as you say, Zandaye," he said. "We can't leave you here alone to suffer the consequences—"

Her head-lamp flamed to a momentary orange. "Suffer the consequences?" she repeated. "By the faith of a Neuter, it is not I that would suffer! It is not myself I was thinking of! I was thinking of you. For I would only have to say you had entered the Desolate Tunnels, and who would there be to blame me? But you—you would pay the penalty!"

"And you, Zandaye, would not suffer at all?"

"Only what I must feel at losing two good friends—and

knowing they would perish. For the Desolate Tunnels are forbidden. They are forbidden because he who goes there can never return. They are cold—so cold that a man would freeze to ice. You will not go there, my friend. Say you will not!"

Even as she spoke, her face was flooded with tears; her head-lamp glowed to a tender blue; and her arms reached out to us imploringly.

However, at that instant, from far down the gallery, we saw a cluster of wavering lights. Realizing how unwise it would be to be seen by any of the natives, we began to act with lightning rapidity. Each of us in turn flung out our arms and for one brief moment held the moist-cheeked Zandaye close against us; then, while she stood lamenting, "My friends, do not go! Do not go! You will be frozen!" we hastily began to leave.

Resorting to a plan that had often served us before, I bent down while Stark—springing to my shoulder—gained a grip on the projecting rim of the upper tunnel. With a powerful tug, he hauled himself to the base of the stairway; then, seizing my hands as I sprang into the air and snatched at the gallery's rocky edge, he pulled and strained mightily, until, in a few seconds, I stood panting safely beside him.

"Goodbye, Zandaye," I called, gazing down upon her sorrowful form.

"Goodbye...goodbye, Zandaye," cried Stark.

"Goodbye, dear friends..." she mourned. "Good-bye. I will never, never forget you. But oh, to think you are going into the Desolate Tunnels—to be frozen..."

The glimmering lights from down the corridor were now growing much brighter. And so, with a last glance back at Zandaye, who stood waving to us while still lamenting, "Oh, my friends, you'll be frozen—you'll be frozen!" Stark and I reluctantly started up the long, dark stairway.

* * *

Since we no longer had our flashlights, hours had passed before we had felt our way to the top of that tremendous, icy flight of steps. Coming out into the open, we found to our joy that no storm was blowing; the stars and the remote, dim sun were shining peacefully through the deep twilight of the frozen plains. Exhilarated at the sight of the heavens and at our first breath of the outer air after the many months of confinement, we began searching for our contragrav car, which had disappeared long before during the tempest, To our relief, it was only a minute before we espied the well-known seventy-foot form looming like a blue-white specter amid the ice-fields a few hundred yards away. Evidently, bewildered by the blizzard, we had wandered in circles after losing the car, and had been within a stone's throw of safety without realizing it.

Although encrusted with ice, the *Wanderer of the Skies* was undamaged. Our food supplies were intact within the sealed interior; our scientific instruments and other equipment had not been harmed. All that we had to do was to scrape the ice from the car; repair the small hole made by the meteorite; gather a few tons of ice for the return trip—and then enter the car, adjust the contragrav screens, and start the gasoline motors…

However, these preliminaries could not be completed for eight or ten days; and meanwhile we feared that the Head Neuter, mastering his dread of the Desolate Tunnels, would send a searching party after us, to capture us and bring us back to justice… However, nothing so tragic occurred, and finally we had the inexpressible pleasure of seeing ourselves rise above the planet's surface…

Seven months later, after an uneventful trip, we returned

to the earth. However, there was an unfortunate miscalculation about our landing, which took us far out of our course and brought us down on a peak of the Canadian Rockies instead of in the eastern United States. The *Wanderer of the Skies*, in the violent descent, was smashed to fragments, and its remains are still to be seen amid the snow and ice of that dismal eminence. But Stark and I were lucky enough to escape with only a few bruises, and eventually made our way back to civilization, although we had not so much as a scrap of paper or a bit of Plutonian clothing to display in testimony of our epoch-making flight. My only memento of the trip is a large bald spot just above the forehead, where my head-lamp checked the growth of hair; while Stark retained a bit of the crystal from his lamp, which, however, was found upon chemical analysis not to differ very much from earthly crystal.

None the less, we are not discouraged. We are planning to construct a larger contragrav car and make a second flight to Pluto as soon as we can collect the necessary two million dollars. We expect that the cost of the expedition will be more than repaid by the gold and precious stones which we shall find in the Afflicted Regions; while at the same time we are drawn an by the thought of a certain blue-eyed young lamp-head, who, we still hope, may be persuaded to break her vows of Pre-Neuterhood and travel with us to the Earth.

THE END

If you've enjoyed this book, you will not want to miss these terrific titles…

ARMCHAIR SCI-FI & HORROR DOUBLE NOVELS, $12.95 each

D-11   **PERIL OF THE STARMEN** by Kris Neville
            THE STRANGE INVASION by Murray Leinster

D-12   **THE STAR LORD** by Boyd Ellanby
            CAPTIVES OF THE FLAME by Samuel R. Delaney

D-13   **MEN OF THE MORNING STAR** by Edmund Hamilton
            PLANET FOR PLUNDER by Hal Clement and Sam Merwin, Jr.

D-14   **ICE CITY OF THE GORGON** by Chester S. Geier and Richard S. Shaver
            WHEN THE WORLD TOTTERED by Lester Del Rey

D-15   **WORLDS WITHOUT END** by Clifford D. Simak
            THE LAVENDER VINE OF DEATH by Don Wilcox

D-16   **SHADOW ON THE MOON** by Joe Gibson
            ARMAGEDDON EARTH by Geoff St. Reynard

D-17   **THE GIRL WHO LOVED DEATH** by Paul W. Fairman
            SLAVE PLANET by Laurence M. Janifer

D-18   **SECOND CHANCE** by J. F. Bone
            MISSION TO A DISTANT STAR by Frank Belknap Long

D-19   **THE SYNDIC** by C. M. Kornbluth
            FLIGHT TO FOREVER by Poul Anderson

D-20   **SOMEWHERE I'LL FIND YOU** by Milton Lesser
            THE TIME ARMADA by Fox B. Holden

ARMCHAIR SCIENCE FICTION CLASSICS, $12.95 each

C-3   **INTO PLUTONIAN DEPTHS**
           by Stanton A. Coblentz

C-4   **CORPUS EARTHLING**
           by Louis Charbonneau

C-5   **THE TIME DISSOLVER**
           by Jerry Sohl

C-6   **WEST OF THE SUN**
           by Edgar Pangborn

ARMCHAIR SCIENCE FICTION & HORROR GEMS SERIES, $12.95 each

G-1   **SCIENCE FICTION GEMS, Vol. One**
           Isaac Asimov and others

G-2   **HORROR GEMS, Vol. One**
           Carl Jacobi and others

12639794R00116

Made in the USA
Charleston, SC
18 May 2012